MAIGRET'S
BOYHOOD
FRIEND

MAIGRET'S BOYHOOD FRIEND

Translated from the French by Eileen Ellenbogen

GEORGES SIMENON

A Helen and Kurt Wolff Book

Harcourt Brace Jovanovich, Inc.

NEW YORK

First edition

ISBN 0–15–155135–9
Library of Congress Catalog Card Number: 79–124825
Printed in the United States of America
Originally published in French under the title
L'Ami d'enfance de Maigret

MAIGRET'S
BOYHOOD
FRIEND

CHAPTER

ONE

The fly circled three times around his head before alighting on the top left-hand corner of the report on which he was making notes.

With pencil poised, Maigret eyed it with amused curiosity. The fly had repeated this maneuver over and over again in the past half-hour. At any rate, Maigret presumed that it was the same fly. It seemed to be the only one in the office.

Each time, it circled once or twice in a patch of sunlight, then buzzed around the Chief Superintendent's head, and finally came to rest on the papers on his desk. And there it stayed for a while, lazily rubbing its legs together and looking at him with an air of defiance.

Was it really looking at him? And if so, what did it take this huge mound of flesh to be—for that was how he must appear to it.

He was at pains not to frighten it away. He sat motionless, with pencil still poised above his papers, until, quite suddenly, the fly took off and vanished through the open window.

It was the middle of June. From time to time a gentle

breeze stirred the air in the office, where Maigret, in shirt sleeves, sat contentedly smoking his pipe. He had set aside this afternoon to read through his inspectors' reports, and was doing so with exemplary patience.

Nine or ten times, the fly had returned to alight on his papers, always on the same spot. It was almost as though it had established a kind of relationship with him.

It was an odd coincidence. The sunshine, the little gusts of cooler air blowing through the window, the intriguing antics of the fly, all served to remind him of his schooldays, when a fly on his desk had often engaged a larger share of his interest than the teacher who had the class.

There was a discreet knock at the door. It was old Joseph, the messenger, bearing an engraved visiting card, which read: *Léon Florentin, Antique Dealer.*

"How old would you say he was?"

"About your age."

"Tall and thin?"

"That's right. Very tall and thin, with a real mop of gray hair."

Yes, that was the man, all right. Florentin, who had been at school with him, at the Lycée Banville in Moulins, the clown of the class.

"Send him in."

He had forgotten the fly, which, feeling slighted perhaps, seemed to have gone for good. There was a brief, embarrassed silence as the two men looked at one another. This was only their second meeting since their school days in Moulins. The first had been a chance encounter in the street about twenty years ago. Florentin, very well groomed, had been accompanied by an attractive and elegant woman.

"This is my old school friend, Maigret. He's a police officer."

Then, to Maigret:

"Allow me to introduce my wife, Monique."

Then, as now, the sun was shining. They had really had nothing to say to one another.

"How are things? Still happy in your work?"

"Yes. And you?"

"Can't complain."

"Are you living in Paris?"

"Yes. Sixty-two Boulevard Haussmann. But I travel a good deal on business. I've just come back from Istanbul. We must get together some time, the two of us, and you and Madame Maigret. . . . I suppose you're married?"

The encounter had been something of an embarrassment to both of them. The couple's pale green, open sports car had been parked nearby, and they had got into it and driven off, leaving Maigret to continue on his way.

The Florentin now facing Maigret across his desk was more seedy than the dashing figure he had seemed to be on the Place de la Madeleine. He was wearing a rather shabby gray suit, and his manner was a good deal less self-assured.

"It was good of you to see me without an appointment. How are you?"

After the first formal greeting, Florentin, a little uneasily, reverted to the *"tu"* of their boyhood. Maigret, somewhat grudgingly, did so too.

"And you? . . . Do sit down. How's your wife?"

For a moment Florentin's pale gray eyes went blank, as though he could not remember.

"Do you mean Monique? The little redhead? It's true we lived together for a time. She was a good sort, but we were never married."

"You're not married, then?"

"What would be the point?"

Florentin made a face. His sharp, well-defined features were so flexible that they might have been made of india rubber. His knack of twisting them into an infinite variety of comical grimaces had been a source of endless amusement to his schoolmates and exasperation to his teachers.

Maigret could not muster the courage to ask what he had come for. He was watching him covertly, finding it hard to believe that it had all been so long ago.

"I like your office. I must admit I never expected to see good furniture in the Law Courts!"

"So you're an antique dealer now?"

"In a manner of speaking. . . . I buy old furniture and do it over. I rent a small workshop on the Boulevard Rochechouart. You know how it is, almost everyone is an antique dealer, nowadays."

"Doing all right, are you?"

"I can't complain. Everything is fine, at least it was until the sky fell around my ears this afternoon."

He was so used to playing the clown that, almost mechanically, his features took on an expression of comical dismay. All the same, his face was gray and his eyes were troubled.

"That's what I came to see you about. I said to myself: He's the only one who'll understand."

He took a pack of cigarettes from his pocket and lit one. His long, bony fingers were trembling slightly. Maigret thought he caught a faint whiff of liquor.

"To tell you the truth, I'm upset . . ."

"Go on."

"That's just the trouble. It's hard to explain. I have a friend, a woman. It's been going on for four years now . . ."

"You and she have been living together?"

"Yes and no. No. Not exactly. . . . She lives on the Rue Notre-Dame-de-Lorette, near the Place Saint-Georges. . . ."

His stammering hesitancy and shifting eyes astonished Maigret. Florentin had been noted for his easy self-assurance. Maigret had always envied him a little on this account, and also because his father had owned the best bakery in the town, facing the cathedral, and Florentin had had a walnut cake named after him. In time, it had become something of a regional specialty.

Florentin had never been short of money. However much he played the clown in class, he was never punished. It was as though he enjoyed a special immunity. And when school was over he used to go out with girls.

"Go on."

"Her name is Josée. Well, actually her real name is Joséphine Papet, but she prefers to be called Josée. . . . I prefer it myself. She's thirty-four, but you'd never think it. . . ."

As he talked, Florentin's mobile face never ceased to change and crease and twitch. It was almost as though he had a nervous tic.

"It's so hard to explain, you know. . . ."

He got up and went over to the window, a tall, sharply etched figure against the sunlight.

"It's hot in here," he sighed, mopping his forehead.

The fly had not returned to its place on the corner of the report on the Chief Superintendent's desk. Cars and buses could be heard rumbling across the Pont Saint-Michel, and from time to time a tug, sounding its siren before lowering its funnel to pass under the bridge.

In Maigret's room, as in every office in Police Headquarters, not to mention all the other Government Departments, there was a black marble clock. The hands stood at twenty past five.

"I'm not the only one . . ." stammered Florentin at last.

"The only what?"

"I'm not Josée's only friend. That's what makes it so hard to explain. She's a marvelous girl . . . the very best. . . . I was everything to her, lover, friend, and confidant. . . ."

Maigret, struggling to contain his impatience, relit his pipe. His old friend returned from the window and resumed his seat opposite him.

After a silence that threatened to become unbearable, the Chief Superintendent ventured a little gentle prompting:

"And she had a good many other friends?"

"Let me think. . . . There was Paré . . . one. . . . And Courcel . . . two. . . . Then there was Victor . . . three. . . . And a youngster known as the redhead—I never saw him . . . that's four."

"Four lovers who visited her regularly?"

"Some once a week, the others twice."

"Did any of them know about the others?"

"Of course not!"

"In other words, each of them was under the delusion that he was keeping her?"

Florentin, nervously tapping the ash of his cigarette onto the carpet, seemed to find this way of putting it embarrassing.

"I told you it was difficult to explain. . . ."

"And where, in all this, do you come in?"

"I'm her friend. . . . I go there when she's alone. . . ."

"Do you sleep at the Rue Notre-Dame-de-Lorette?"

"Every night except Thursdays."

Maigret, trying not to sound sardonic, asked:

"Because that's someone else's night?"

"Yes, Courcel's. . . . She's known him ten years. . . . He lives in Rouen, but he has business premises on the Boulevard Voltaire. . . . It would take too long to explain. . . . I daresay you despise me for it. . . ."

"I've never despised anyone in my life."

"I realize it's a delicate situation, and that most people would frown on it. . . . But you have my solemn word for it, Josée and I love each other. . . ." Abruptly, he added: "Or rather, I should say, loved each other."

Though careful to avoid showing it, Maigret was shaken by this use of the past tense.

"Are you saying that you've broken with her?"

"No."

"Is she dead?"

"Yes."

"When did she die?"

"This afternoon. . . ."

And Florentin, looking him straight in the face, said, in a tragic manner that Maigret could not help feeling was somewhat theatrical:

"I swear it wasn't me. . . . You know me. . . . It's because you know me, and I know you, that I've come to you."

True, they had known each other at twelve, at fifteen, at seventeen, but they had long since parted and gone their separate ways.

"How did she die?"

"She was shot."

"By whom?"

"I don't know."

"Where did it happen?"

"In her apartment . . . her bedroom. . . ."

"Where were you at the time?"

Maigret was finding it more and more awkward to use the informal "*tu.*"

"In the wardrobe."

"In her apartment, you mean?"

"Yes. . . . It wasn't the first time. . . . Whenever I was there, and the bell rang, I . . . it sounds despicable to you,

I daresay . . . but I swear it wasn't like that. . . . I work for my living. . . . I earn . . ."

"Try to describe exactly what happened."

"Where shall I begin?"

"At midday, let's say."

"We had lunch together. She's a marvelous cook. . . . We were sitting over by the window. . . . She was expecting someone, as always on a Wednesday, but not before five thirty to six. . . ."

"Who was it?"

"His name is François Paré. He's a man in his early fifties, head of a Department in the Ministry of Public Works. . . . He's in charge of Waterways. . . . He lives at Versailles. . . ."

"Did he never arrive early?"

"No."

"What happened after lunch?"

"We chatted."

"How was she dressed?"

"In her dressing gown. . . . Except when she was going out, she always wore a dressing gown. . . . It was about half past three when the bell rang, and I took refuge in the wardrobe. . . . It's a sort of closet really . . . in the bathroom, not the bedroom. . . ."

Maigret was beginning to find all this a little wearing.

"And then what?"

"I'd been in there about a quarter of an hour when I heard a sound like a shot."

"That would have been at about a quarter to four?"

"I imagine so."

"So you rushed into the bedroom?"

"No. . . . I wasn't supposed to be there. . . . Besides, it might not have been a shot, but just a car or a bus backfiring."

The whole of Maigret's attention was now focused on Florentin. He recalled that in the old days most of the tales he told were pure fantasy, almost as though he had been unable to distinguish between lies and truth.

"What were you waiting for?" Without realizing it, Maigret had addressed him as *vous*.

"Why so formal? . . . Don't you see?"

Florentin looked hurt and disappointed.

"Sorry, no offense meant. What were you waiting for, there in the wardrobe?"

"It's not a wardrobe, really—more of a large clothes closet. I was waiting for the man to go."

"How do you know it was a man? You didn't see him, you say. . . ."

Florentin looked stunned.

"I never thought of that!"

"Was it because Josée had no women friends?"

"As a matter of fact, I don't think she did. . . ."

"Any family?"

"She came from Concarneau originally. I never met any of her family."

"How did you know when the caller had gone?"

"I heard footsteps in the living room, and the door opening and closing."

"What time was that?"

"About four."

"So the murderer was there about a quarter of an hour after he killed her?"

"I suppose he must have been."

"When you went into the bedroom, where did you find her?"

"On the floor, next to the bed."

"How was she dressed?"

"She was still wearing her yellow dressing gown."

"Where was she shot?"

"In the throat."

"Are you sure she was dead?"

"There couldn't be any doubt about that."

"What was the state of the room?"

"Much as usual. . . . I didn't notice anything wrong."

"Any drawers left open . . . papers scattered about?"

"No, I don't think so."

"You mean you can't be sure?"

"I was too upset. . . ."

"Did you call a doctor?"

"No. . . . Seeing that she was already dead . . ."

"Did you call the local police?"

"No. . . . I . . ."

"You got here at five past five. . . . What had you been doing since four o'clock?"

"To begin with, I was absolutely stunned. . . . I just collapsed into an armchair. . . . I couldn't understand it. . . . I still can't. . . . Then I realized that I was the one they'd be bound to suspect . . . especially as that bitch of a concierge can't stand the sight of me."

"Are you telling me that you sat there for the best part of an hour?"

"No. . . . I don't know how long it was, but eventually I pulled myself together and went into a bistro, the Grand-Saint-Georges, and had three large brandies, one after another."

"And then?"

"And then I remembered that you are now the Big White Chief of the Criminal Investigation Department."

"How did you get here?"

"I took a taxi."

Maigret was furious, but his expression remained impassive. He went across to the door leading to the inspectors' duty room, opened it, and looked uncertainly from Janvier to Lapointe, who were both at their desks. Finally, addressing Janvier, he said:

"Come in here a minute, will you? I want you to call Moers, at the lab, and ask him to join us on the Rue Notre-Dame-de-Lorette. . . . What number?"

"Seventeen B."

Each time his glance rested on his old school friend, Maigret's eyes hardened in an expression of impenetrable reserve. As Janvier was telephoning, he glanced at the clock. It was half past five.

"What did you say his name was, the Wednesday visitor?"

"Paré. . . . The civil servant. . . ."

"Ordinarily, you'd be expecting him to arrive at the apartment about now?"

"That's right. . . . He'd be due just about now. . . ."

"Has he got a key?"

"None of them have keys."

"Have you a key?"

"That's quite a different matter. Don't you see, my friend . . ."

"I'd rather you didn't address me as your friend."

"There, you see! Even you . . ."

"Let's be going."

He grabbed his hat on the way out, and as they descended the wide, grayish stone staircase he refilled his pipe.

"What I want to know is why it took you so long to make up your mind to come and see me. . . . And why didn't you get in touch with the local police? Did she have any money of her own?"

"I imagine so. . . . Three or four years ago she bought a

— 13 —

house as an investment, on the Rue du Mont-Cenis, overlooking Montmartre."

"Did she keep any money in the apartment?"

"She may have, I can't say. . . . What I do know is that she distrusted banks."

They got into one of the row of little black cars parked in the forecourt, with Janvier at the wheel.

"Are you saying that, all the time you were living with her, you never found out where she kept her savings?"

"It's the truth."

It was all he could do to prevent himself from bursting out: "Stop playing the clown, can't you!"

Was it pity that he felt for him?

"How many rooms are there in the apartment?"

"Living room, dining room, bedroom, bathroom, and small kitchen."

"Not to mention the clothes closet."

"And the clothes closet."

Weaving his way through the traffic, Janvier tried to pick up the threads from these snatches of overheard conversation.

"I swear to you, Maigret . . ."

It was something to be thankful for that he did not address him as "Jules." Fortunately, it had been customary at the lycée for the boys to call one another by their surnames.

As the three men went past the glass-walled lodge, Maigret saw the net curtain over the door twitch, and caught a glimpse of the concierge. She was, in every sense, a huge woman, massively built and enormously fat. Her face was large, round, and expressionless, and, staring at them, she resembled a larger-than-life statue or oil painting.

The elevator was cramped, and Maigret, crushed up against Florentin, found himself almost eyeball to eyeball with his old school friend. He felt thoroughly uncomfortable. What thoughts were, at this moment, passing through the mind of the baker's son from Moulins? He was making an effort to appear natural, even to smile, but was succeeding only in screwing up his face into a ludicrous grimace. Was he frightened, was that it?

Was he the murderer of Joséphine Papet? What had he been up to during the hour that had elapsed before his arrival at the Quai des Orfèvres?

On the third floor they crossed the hallway, and Florentin took a bunch of keys out of his pocket, as though it were the most natural thing in the world. The door of the apartment opened onto a tiny entrance hall, and Florentin led them straight into the living room. Maigret felt as though he had been transported back fifty years or more.

The elaborately draped curtains were of old rose silk, held back by heavy braided silk cords. A faded, flowered carpet covered the parquet floor. There was a great deal of plush and brocade upholstery, a number of table runners, and, on all the fake Louis XVI chairs, antimacassars of lace or embroidery.

Near the window stood a velvet-covered sofa, piled high with crumpled cushions of every color, as though someone had very recently been sitting there. On a pedestal table nearby, there was a gilt table lamp with a pink shade.

This, no doubt, had been Josée's favorite seat. There was a record player within easy reach, a box of chocolates, and a handy pile of magazines and romantic novels. The television set stood facing the sofa, in the opposite corner of the room.

The walls were papered in a pattern of tiny flowers, and here and there were landscape paintings crowded with fussy detail.

Florentin, who was watching Maigret closely, confirmed his impression:

"That's where she nearly always sat."

"What about you?"

The antique dealer pointed to a shabby leather armchair, which looked entirely out of place in such a setting.

"That's mine. I brought it here for my own use."

The dining room was no less conventionally old-fashioned, and conveyed the same impression of overcrowded stuffiness. There were heavy, draped, velvet curtains over both windows, and dark green potted plants on the sills.

The door to the bedroom was open. As Florentin seemed reluctant to go in, Maigret pushed past him. The body was stretched out on the carpet, not six feet from the door.

As so often happens in such cases, the hole in the woman's throat seemed much larger than might have been expected from a bullet wound. She had bled a great deal, but her face expressed nothing but pure astonishment.

As far as one could judge, she must have been a plump, kindly little woman, the sort usually associated with good home cooking, nourishing stews, and lovingly put-up preserves.

Maigret's glance traveled around the room, as though searching for something that appeared to be missing.

"There was no weapon as far as I could see. . . ." His friend was quick to guess what he was looking for. "Unless she's lying on it, which doesn't seem very likely."

The telephone was in the living room. Maigret was anxious to get the necessary formalities over and done with as quickly as possible.

"You'd better call the Divisional Superintendent first, Janvier. Tell him to bring a pathologist. . . . After that, let the Public Prosecutor's office know. . . ."

Moers and his staff of experts would be arriving any minute now. Maigret would have liked a few quiet minutes to himself.

He went into the bathroom and noted that all the towels were pink. There was a great deal of pink all over the apartment. He opened the door of the clothes closet, which was a kind of short passage, leading nowhere. Here was more pink, a sugar-pink negligée and a summer dress of a deeper pink. Indeed, all the clothes hanging there were of pastel colors, mostly almond green and powder blue.

"There doesn't seem to be anything of yours here."

"It would have made things a bit awkward," murmured Florentin, more than a little put out. "There were the others, you see. . . . Ostensibly, she was living alone. . . ."

Naturally! There was an old-fashioned flavor about this too: a succession of elderly "protectors," who came once or twice a week, each unaware of the existence of the others, and fondly cherishing the illusion that he was "keeping" her.

But had she really succeeded in keeping all of them in ignorance?

Returning to the bedroom, Maigret began poking about in various drawers. He found bills, underclothes, and a jewelry box containing a few cheap trinkets.

It was six o'clock.

"The Wednesday caller ought to be here by now," he remarked.

"He could have been and gone. If he rang and got no answer, he wouldn't have hung about, would he?"

Janvier came in from the living room.

"The Superintendent is on his way, and the Assistant Public Prosecutor will be arriving shortly with the Examining Magistrate."

In any inquiry, this was always the stage that Maigret most detested, with half a dozen of them sitting about staring at one another, while the police doctor knelt by the corpse, making his examination.

It was a pure formality, anyway. The doctor could do no more than confirm death. For the details, they would have to await the autopsy. As for the Assistant Public Prosecutor, he also confirmed death in the name of the Government.

The Examining Magistrate was looking at Maigret as though seeking his opinion, whereas, of course, Maigret had, so far, not formed any opinion. As for the Divisional Superintendent, he was all impatience to get back to his office.

"Keep me in the picture," murmured the Examining Magistrate. He was a man of about forty, and must only recently have come to Paris.

His name was Page. He had worked his way up from an obscure provincial post, through most of the major provincial cities, to his present appointment in the capital.

Moers and his men were waiting in the living room, where one of them was examining all likely surfaces for fingerprints.

When he had seen the official party off the premises, Maigret said to Moers: "It's all yours. You'd better get on with photographing the body before the hearse arrives."

Seeing that Florentin evidently intended to follow him out, he said:

"No, you stay here. Janvier, I'll leave you to interview the neighbors on this floor, and, if necessary, those on the floor above. You never know, they may have heard something."

The Chief Superintendent, ignoring the elevator, went down by the stairs. The house was old, but very well cared for. The crimson carpet was secured by brass stair rods. All the doorknobs were highly polished, and beside the door of one of the apartments was a gleaming brass plate, inscribed: "Mademoiselle Vial. Corsets and foundation garments made to measure."

The giantess of a concierge was still standing behind the glass door of the lodge, holding back the net curtain with the bloated fingers of her huge hand. As he put his hand on the doorknob, she moved back a pace, as though pushed, and he went in.

She looked at him with such a total lack of interest that he might have been an object rather than a person; nor did his official badge, when he produced it, evoke the slightest response.

"I take it you haven't heard?"

She did not reply, but her eyes seemed to ask: "Haven't heard what?"

The lodge was spotlessly clean, with a round table in the center, on which stood a cage containing two canaries. The kitchen could be seen through a door at the far end.

"Mademoiselle Papet is dead."

This at least did elicit some response. She did have a tongue, it seemed, though her voice was toneless, as blank as her face. But maybe she was not as indifferent as she appeared. Was not that very blankness possibly evidence of hostility? It was as though she looked out upon humanity through her wall of glass, hating all she saw.

"Is that what all the coming and going is about? There must be ten or a dozen people up there still, I should think."

"What's your name?"

"I can't see what business it is of yours."

"As I shall have to put a number of questions to you, I shall need your name to include in my report."

"Madame Blanc."

"Widow?"

"No."

"Does your husband live here with you?"

"No."

"Did he desert you?"

"Nineteen years ago."

In the end she condescended to sit down, in a huge armchair that must have been specially made for her. Maigret, too, sat down.

"Did you see anyone go up to Mademoiselle Papet's apartment between half past five and six?"

"Yes, at twenty to six."

"Who was it?"

"The Wednesday regular, of course. I don't know their names. He's tall, going bald, and always wears a dark suit."

"Was he up there long?"

"No."

"Did he say anything when he came down?"

"He asked me if her highness had gone out."

He had to draw the information out of her, a very little at a time.

"What did you say?"

"That I hadn't seen her."

"Did he seem surprised?"

"Yes."

It was exhausting, especially with that blank, fixed stare to contend with. Her eyes were as motionless as her gross body.

"Did you see him earlier in the day?"

"No."

"Did you see anyone go up around half past three? Were you here then?"

"I was here, but no one went up."

"Did you see anyone come down, around four o'clock?"

"Not till twenty past four. . . ."

"Who was that?"

"That fellow."

"Whom do you mean by 'that fellow'?"

"The one who was with you. . . . I can't bring myself to call him by his name."

"Joséphine Papet's real lover, you mean?"

That did bring a smile to her lips, a smile at once ironic and embittered.

"Did he speak to you?"

"I wouldn't even go so far as to open the door for him."

"Are you quite sure no one else went up or came down between half past three and four?"

Having already said so, she was not prepared to go to the trouble of repeating herself.

"Do you know your tenant's other friends?"

"Friends! Is that what you call them?"

"Visitors, then. How many of them are there?"

Her lips moved, as though in prayer. At last she said:

"Four, not counting that fellow."

"Did any of them ever meet? Was there ever any trouble?"

"Not that I know of."

"Are you in here all day, every day?"

"Except in the morning, when I go out to do my marketing, or when I'm cleaning the stairs."

"Did you, yourself, have any visitors today?"

"I never have any visitors."

"Did Mademoiselle Papet go out much?"

"Usually at about eleven in the morning, just around the corner to do her marketing. Occasionally she went to the movies in the evening, with *him*."

"What about Sunday?"

"Sometimes they went out in the car."

"Whose car?"

"Hers, of course."

"Did she drive?"

"No, he did."

"Do you know where the car is now?"

"In a garage on the Rue La Bruyère."

She did not ask him what had caused her tenant's death. She was as devoid of curiosity as of energy. Maigret looked at her with growing wonder.

"Mademoiselle Papet was murdered."

"Well, it was only to be expected, wasn't it?"

"Why do you say that?"

"Well, with all those men . . ."

"She was shot almost at point-blank range."

She nodded, but said nothing.

"Did she never confide in you?"

"She was no friend of mine."

"In other words, you couldn't stand her."

"I wouldn't go as far as that."

It was becoming oppressive. Maigret mopped his forehead and made his escape. It was a great relief to be outside in the open air. The hearse from the Pathologists' Laboratory had just arrived. He would only be in the way while the men were bringing down the body on a stretcher. He decided to go across the road to the Grand-Saint-Georges and have a pint of beer at the bar.

The murder of Joséphine Papet had not caused the faintest stir in the neighborhood, not even in the house where she had lived for so many years.

He watched the hearse drive away. As he went back into the house, he saw the concierge standing watching him exactly as before. He went up in the elevator and rang the doorbell. Janvier let him in.

"Have you seen the neighbors?"

"Those that were at home. There are three apartments to every floor, two overlooking the street and one the yard at the back. Mademoiselle Papet's nearest neighbor is a Madame Sauveur, an elderly woman, very pleasant, very well groomed. She was in all afternoon, knitting and listening to the radio.

"She heard a sound that might have been a muffled shot about midafternoon, but she thought it was a car or bus backfiring."

"Didn't she hear anyone going in or leaving?"

"I checked that. You can't hear the door opening or shutting from her apartment. It's quite an old building, and the walls are thick."

"What about upstairs?"

"There's a couple with two children. They've been away in the country or at the seaside for the past week. . . . The apartment at the back belongs to a retired railway official. He has his grandson living with him. He didn't hear a thing."

Florentin was standing at the open window.

The Chief Superintendent asked him:

"Was that window open earlier this afternoon?"

"I think so. . . . Yes."

"What about the bedroom window?"

"No, I'm sure it wasn't."

"How can you be so positive?"

"Because Josée was always very careful to keep it shut when she had a visitor."

Across from the bedroom window could be seen a spacious dressmaker's workroom, with a dress form covered in coarse canvas, mounted on a black base, and four or five teen-age girls sewing.

Florentin, though making a visible effort to keep smiling, seemed uneasy. That fixed, forced smile reminded Maigret of the old days at the Lycée Banville, when, as often happened, Florentin was caught mimicking a teacher behind his back.

"You won't allow us to forget that we are descended from the apes, I see, Master Florentin," the weedy little fair-haired man who taught them Latin used to say.

Moers and his men were going through the apartment with

a fine-tooth comb. Nothing, not so much as a speck of dust, escaped them. In spite of the open window, Maigret was feeling the heat. This case was not at all to his liking. There was something distasteful about it. Besides, he felt that he had been placed in a false position, and he was finding it impossible wholly to banish the past from his mind.

He had completely lost touch with all his old school friends, and now here was one turning up out of the blue, in a predicament that was delicate, to say the least.

"Have you seen our piece of monumental masonry?"

Maigret looked puzzled.

"The concierge. That's what I call her. I shudder to think what she calls me."

" 'That fellow.' "

"So I'm 'that fellow,' am I? What else did she say about me?"

"You're sure you've told me everything, exactly as it occurred?"

"Why should I lie to you?"

"You were always a liar. You lied for the fun of it."

"That was forty years ago!"

"You don't strike me has having changed so much."

"If I had had anything to hide, would I have deliberately sought you out?"

"What else could you have done?"

"I could have made a run for it. . . . I could have gone back to my apartment on the Boulevard Rochechouart."

"To wait there until I came the following morning to arrest you?"

"I could have left the country."

"Have you got any money?"

Florentin flushed crimson, and Maigret felt a twinge of pity for him. As a young boy he had been a kind of licensed jester, with his long clownish face, his jokes, and his grimaces. But in an older man the youthful mannerisms were no longer entertaining. Indeed, they were painful to watch.

"You surely don't imagine that I killed her?"

"Why not?"

"But you know me. . . ."

"The last time I set eyes on you was twenty years ago, on the Place de la Madeleine, and that, if you remember, was our first meeting since we were schoolboys in Moulins."

"Do I look like a murderer?"

"A man may be a blameless citizen one minute and a murderer the next. Up to the moment of his victim's death, he is a man like any other."

"Why should I have killed her? We were the greatest of friends."

"Just friends?"

"Of course not, but I'm rather past the age for a grand passion."

"What about her?"

"I believe she loved me."

"Was she jealous?"

"I never gave her cause to be. . . . You still haven't told me what that old witch downstairs has been saying."

Janvier was intrigued by the situation, which was unusual, to say the least. He was watching the Chief Superintendent closely, curious to see how he would handle it. Maigret was plainly hesitant and uneasy. For one thing, he seemed unable to make up his mind whether to address Florentin as *"tu"* or *"vous."*

"She didn't see anyone go upstairs."

"She's lying. If not, the man must have slipped past the lodge while she was in the kitchen. . . ."

"She denies that she ever left the lodge."

"But that's impossible! The man who killed her must have come from somewhere. . . . Unless . . ."

"Unless what?"

"Unless he was in the house already."

"One of the tenants?"

Florentin seized upon this suggestion eagerly.

"Why not? I'm not the only man in the building."

"Was Josée friendly with any of the other tenants?"

"How should I know? I wasn't here all the time. I have my own business to attend to. I work for my living. . . ."

This statement had the unmistakable ring of falsehood. Florentin, who had spent his whole life acting some part or other, now saw himself in the role of breadwinner.

"Janvier, I'll leave you to comb the building from top to bottom. Call at all the apartments. Talk to everyone you can. I'm going back to the Quai. . . ."

"What about the car?"

Maigret had never been able to bring himself to learn to drive.

"I'll take a taxi."

And, turning to Florentin, he said:

"You come with me."

"You're not arresting me, surely?"

"No."

"What are you up to, then? What do you want me for?"

"Just for a chat."

CHAPTER
TWO

Maigret's original intention had been to take Florentin back with him to the Quai des Orfèvres, but just as he was about to give the address to the taxi driver he changed his mind.

"What number Boulevard Rochechouart?" he asked Florentin.

"Fifty-five B. Why?"

"Fifty-five B Boulevard Rochechouart," Maigret said to the taxi driver.

It was no distance. The driver, annoyed at having been engaged for so short a trip, grumbled under his breath.

Sandwiched between a picture framer and a tobacconist-cum-bar was a narrow cobbled alley leading to two glass-fronted workshops, outside one of which stood a handcart. Inside the other, a painter was at work on a view of the Sacré-Coeur, which was no doubt intended for the tourist trade. Judging from the way in which he was dashing it off, he must have produced them by the dozen. He had long hair and a pepper-and-salt beard, and he wore a floppy bow tie of the kind favored by pseudo-artists at the turn of the century.

Florentin got out his bunch of keys and unlocked the door of the workshop on the right. Maigret followed him inside, burning with resentment.

For Florentin had somehow contrived to tarnish his boyhood memories. At the very moment when he had turned up at the Quai des Orfèvres, Maigret had been watching the fly that had settled so obstinately on the top left-hand corner of the report he was studying, and reliving his school days in Moulins.

What, he had wondered, had become of the other boys in his class? He had completely lost touch with all of them. Crochet, whose father had been a notary, had presumably taken over his practice by now. Orban, plump and good-natured, had, no doubt, achieved his ambition and qualified as a doctor. As for the others, they had probably settled in various towns all over France, or gone to live abroad.

Why, among them all, did it have to be Florentin to cross his path, and in such very disagreeable circumstances, at that?

He had a vivid recollection of the baker's shop, though he had seldom been in it. For some of the other boys, those with money to spare, it had been a meeting place, where they ate ices and cakes in an atmosphere redolent of hot spices and sugar, surrounded by marble and gilt-framed mirrors. According to the knowing ladies of the town, a cake was not worth having unless it came from Florentin's.

Returning to the present, he found himself in a dark, dusty room, full of junk, with windows that looked as though they had never been cleaned, and which consequently let in very little light.

"I'm sorry about the mess. . . ."

In the circumstances, for Florentin to call himself an antique dealer was worse than pretentious. God knows where he had got the furniture that was lying about the place, but it was all alike, old, battered, ugly, and quite worthless. The most that could be done with it was to repair the worst of the damage, and slightly improve its appearance with furniture polish.

"Have you been in this business long?"

"Three years."

"And before that?"

"I was in exports."

"What did you export?"

"A little of everything. Chiefly to the emergent countries of Africa."

"And before that?"

It was a humiliating question. Florentin murmured uncomfortably:

"Oh well, you know, this and that. . . . I tried my hand at all sorts of things. I had no wish to spend the rest of my days in the shop in Moulins. My sister married a baker, and they are running the business now."

Maigret remembered Florentin's sister, plump as a pigeon behind the snow-white counter of the shop. Had he not been just a little in love with her? She was fresh-faced and cheerful, like her mother, whom she closely resembled.

"Living in Paris, one has to use one's wits. . . . I've had my ups and downs. . . ."

Maigret had known so many like him, up one minute, down the next, forever promoting some marvelously profitable scheme, which, in the end, collapsed like a house of cards. Such men were always within a hairsbreadth of arrest and imprisonment. Frequently, though they might try to touch you for a loan of a hundred thousand francs to build a seaport in some remote territory, they would gladly settle for a hundred francs, to avoid the indignity of being thrown out of their lodgings.

Florentin had been lucky. He had found Josée. If the workshop was anything to go by, it was evident that he could not be making a living out of selling furniture.

There was a door at the back. It was ajar. Maigret pushed it open, to reveal a narrow, windowless room, bare except for an iron bedstead, a washstand, and a rickety wardrobe.

"Is this where you sleep?"

"Only on Thursdays."

Maigret could not now remember who the Thursday caller was, the only one privileged to spend the night on the Rue Notre-Dame-de-Lorette.

"Fernand Courcel," volunteered Florentin. "He and Josée were friends long before I came on the scene. . . . He's been coming to see her and taking her out for the past ten years. . . . He can't get away nowadays as much as he used to, but he still manages to find an excuse for spending Thursday nights in Paris. . . ."

Maigret was poking about in corners, opening hideous old cupboards, from which all the varnish had been scratched and worn away. He was not at all sure what he was looking for, only that something was bothering him, some detail that had escaped him.

"You did say, didn't you, that Josée had no bank account?"

"Yes. At least, as far as I know."

"You say she mistrusted banks?"

"That was part of it. . . . But mainly she didn't want anyone to know what she had, because of tax . . ."

Maigret came upon an old pipe.

"Do you smoke a pipe?"

"Not in her apartment. She disliked the smell. . . . Only when I'm here. . . ."

In one crude country-style wardrobe there were some clothes, a blue suit, some shabby jeans, three or four shirts, espadrilles thick with sawdust, and one solitary pair of outdoor shoes.

The wardrobe of a filthy bum. Joséphine Papet must have had money. Had she been mean with it, mistrustful of Florentin, who would not have hesitated to squander it all, down to the last sou?

He had found nothing of interest, and almost regretted having come. After all he had seen, he was beginning to feel sorry for his old school friend. As he was making for the door, he caught sight of something that was wrapped in newspaper on top of a cupboard. He turned back, took a chair up to the cupboard, climbed onto it, and lifted down a square parcel.

Florentin's forehead was beaded with perspiration.

The Chief Superintendent removed the wrappings to reveal a tin biscuit box, with the maker's name stamped on it in red and yellow. He opened it. It was tightly packed with bundles of hundred-franc notes.

"Those are my savings. . . ."

Maigret stared at him blankly, as though he had not heard. He sat down at the workbench to count the bundles of notes. There were forty-eight.

"Are you fond of biscuits?"

"I like one occasionally."

"Have you got another box like this?"

"Not at the moment, I don't think . . ."

"There were two, I noticed, of the same make, in the apartment on the Rue Notre-Dame-de-Lorette."

"I daresay that's where I got it. . . ."

He had always been a liar, either because he couldn't help himself, or just for the fun of it. He was forever inventing, and the more unlikely the tale, the more barefaced the lies he told. This time, however, there was a great deal at stake.

"Now I see why you didn't get to the Quai des Orfèvres before five."

"I couldn't make up my mind what to do. . . . I was frightened. I knew that I was bound to come under suspicion. . . ."

"You came here."

He still persisted in denying it, but his self-confidence was ebbing fast.

"If you won't tell me, the painter next door will."

"You must listen to me, Maigret."

His lower lip was trembling. He seemed on the verge of bursting into tears. It was a distressing sight.

"I know I don't always tell the truth. I can't help myself. Don't you remember how I used to have you all in fits of laughter with the tales I made up to amuse you? But you've got to believe me now, I beg of you. I didn't kill Josée, and I truly was hiding in the clothes closet when it happened."

He really was a pathetic sight, but then it should not be forgotten that he was also a born actor.

"If I had killed her, would I have come to you, of all people?"

"In that case, why didn't you tell me the truth?"

"I don't know what you mean. What truth?"

He was prevaricating, playing for time.

"At three o'clock this afternoon, this biscuit box was still in the apartment on the Rue Notre-Dame-de-Lorette. Isn't that so?"

"Yes."

"Well, then?"

"Surely it's not so hard to understand. . . . Josée had completely lost touch with her family. . . . She had only one sister, married to a fruit grower in Morocco. They're rich people. I'm on my uppers, so, when I saw her lying there, dead . . ."

"You took advantage of the situation to make off with the loot."

"That's a crude way of putting it, but just look at it from my point of view. After all, I wasn't doing any harm to anyone. . . . And without her, I didn't know what was to become of me."

Maigret looked fixedly at him, a prey to conflicting emotions.

"Come along."

He was hot and thirsty. He felt utterly exhausted, fed up with himself and everyone else.

As they emerged from the little alley, he hesitated for a moment, then propelled his companion into the tobacconist's shop that was also a bar.

He ordered two beers.

"Do you or don't you believe me?"

"We'll talk about it later."

Maigret drank two beers, then set about looking for a taxi. It was the rush hour, and the traffic was at its worst. It took them half an hour to get to the Quai des Orfèvres. The sky was a uniform blue. It was oppressively close. All the café terraces were crowded, and there were men in shirt sleeves everywhere, carrying their jackets.

His office, from which the sun had by now retreated, was comparatively cool.

"Take a seat. . . . Smoke if you feel like it."

"Thanks. . . . It's a very odd feeling, you know, to find oneself in a situation like this with an old school friend."

"Don't I know it!" grumbled the Chief Superintendent, refilling his pipe.

"It's different for you."

"Well . . ."

"You take a pretty low view of me, don't you? To you, I'm just a slob."

"It's not for me to pass judgment. I'm trying to understand."

"I loved her."

"I see."

"I don't pretend it was a grand passion. We didn't claim to be Romeo and Juliet. . . ."

"I must admit I can't quite see Romeo skulking in a clothes closet. Was that a regular occurrence?"

"No, not more than three or four times. . . . It was most unusual for any of them to call unexpectedly. . . ."

"Did these gentlemen know of your existence?"

"Of course not!"

"Did you never meet any of them?"

"I knew them by sight. . . . I couldn't help wondering what they looked like, so I hung about in the street, waiting for them to come out. I'm being perfectly frank with you, you see. . . ."

"Have you never been tempted to try a little blackmail? They're all married men, I presume, fathers of families, and so on?"

"I swear to you . . ."

"You're altogether too ready to swear to anything. I wish you wouldn't . . ."

"Very well, but how else can I make you believe me?"

"By telling the truth."

"I never resorted to blackmail."

"Why not?"

"I was happy with things as they were. I'm not young any more. I've been a rolling stone long enough. All I wanted was a quiet life and a bit of security. It was restful being with Josée, and she took good care of me."

"Whose idea was it to buy a car? Yours?"

"No, we both wanted one. I may have been the first to suggest it. . . ."

"Where did you go on Sundays?"

"Nowhere in particular . . . anywhere—the Chevreuse Valley . . . the Forest of Fontainebleau . . . occasionally, though not often, we'd have a day by the sea. . . ."

"Did you know where she kept her money?"

"She made no secret of it, as far as I was concerned. She trusted me. For heaven's sake, Maigret, what possible reason could I have had to kill her?"

"Suppose she was tired of you?"

"But she wasn't! Quite the opposite, in fact. The whole point of saving money was so that eventually we could set up house together somewhere in the country. Put yourself in my place. . . ."

Chief Superintendent or not, it was Maigret's turn to make a face.

"Do you own a revolver?"

"She had one that she always kept in the drawer of her bedside table. It was very old. I found it a couple of years ago in a chest I bought at an auction."

"Was there any ammunition with it?"

"If you mean was it loaded, yes, it was."

"And you kept it at the Rue Notre-Dame-de-Lorette?"

"Josée was rather a nervous type. I thought it would reassure her to have it close at hand in the bedside table drawer."

"It isn't there now."

"I know. I looked for it, too."

"Why?"

"I realize it was stupid of me. . . . I've behaved like an idiot. . . . The trouble with me is that I just blurt everything out. . . . I should have phoned the local police and stayed put until they arrived. . . . I could have told them any old tale—that I'd just arrived and found her dead. . . ."

"I asked you a straight question and I want a straight answer. Why were you looking for the revolver?"

"To get rid of it. . . . I would have shoved it down a drain, or thrown it in the river. . . . Since it was my gun, I realized it was bound to get me into trouble. . . .

"And how right I was, seeing that even you . . ."

"So far, I haven't accused you of anything."

"But the reason I'm here is that you don't believe a word I say. . . . Am I under arrest?"

Maigret looked at him uncertainly. He appeared grave and anxious.

"No," he said, at last.

He was taking a risk, and he knew it, but he didn't have the heart to do otherwise.

"Where do you intend to go from here?"

"I'll have to get a bite to eat, I suppose, and after that I'll just go to bed."

"Where?"

Florentin hesitated.

"I don't know. . . . I suppose I'd better keep away from the Rue Notre-Dame-de-Lorette. . . ."

Was he really so insensitive as to be in any doubt about it?

"Oh well, it'll just have to be the Boulevard Rochechouart."

In the narrow little windowless box at the back of the workshop, where there weren't even any sheets on the bed, only a shabby, old, threadbare, gray blanket.

Maigret got up and went into the inspectors' duty room. Lapointe was on the telephone. He waited until he had finished.

"I've got a man in my office, tall and thin, my age, but pretty seedy. He lives at the end of a little alley off the Boulevard Rochechouart, Number Fifty-five B. . . . I don't know what he'll do when he leaves here, but I don't want you to let him out of your sight.

"See to it that there's someone to relieve you on the night shift. . . .

"And arrange for someone else to take over in the morning."

"Does it matter if he knows he's being followed?"

"Better not, but it's not very important. . . . He's as cunning as a barrelful of monkeys, and he's sure to be on the lookout. . . ."

"I'll see to it, sir. . . . I'd better go and wait for him outside."

"I shan't keep him more than another minute or two."

As Maigret pushed open the door, Florentin stepped back several paces, looking thoroughly uncomfortable.

"So you were listening?"

Florentin hesitated, then the corners of his wide mouth twitched in a rather pathetic smile.

"What would you have done in my place?"

"You heard, then?"

"Not everything. . . ."

"I'm having you tailed by one of my inspectors. I warn you that if you make any attempt to shake him off, I'll put out an all-stations call and you'll find yourself under lock and key."

"There's no need to speak to me like that, Maigret!"

Much as the Chief Superintendent would have liked to tell

him to stop addressing him in that familiar way, he didn't have the heart to do so.

"Where were you planning to go?"

"When?"

"You knew that there would be an investigation, and that you were bound to be a suspect. It wasn't very sensible of you to hide the money where you did. . . . Presumably you intended to move it somewhere safer as soon as you got the chance. . . . Had you already decided to come to me?"

"No, my first thought was to go to the local police."

"You didn't consider leaving the country before the body was found?"

"It did cross my mind."

"What stopped you?"

"I realized it would look like an admission of guilt, and I'd be laying myself open to extradition, so, on second thoughts, I decided to go to the local police . . . and then, suddenly, I remembered about you. . . . I'd seen your name in the papers, often. You're the only one in our class to have become almost a celebrity."

Maigret was still contemplating his old school friend with an air of perplexity, as though he represented an insoluble problem.

"You have the reputation of not being taken in by appearances. They say that you worry a thing until you get to the bottom of it, so I was hoping you'd understand. . . . I'm beginning to think I was mistaken. . . . You believe I'm guilty, and you might as well admit it."

"I've already told you, I haven't made up my mind one way or the other."

"I shouldn't have taken the money. I did it on an impulse. . . . It didn't even occur to me to take it until I was actually on my way out. . . ."

"You may go."

They were both on their feet. Florentin hesitated, as though about to hold out his hand. Perhaps in order to forestall him, Maigret got out his handkerchief and mopped his face.

"Shall I be seeing you tomorrow?"

"Very likely."

"Good-by, Maigret."

"Good-by."

He did not stand at the door to watch him as he went down the stairs, with Lapointe at his heels.

For no very precise reason, Maigret was displeased with himself. With himself and everyone else. Up to five o'clock things had jogged along at an agreeably indolent pace. He had enjoyed his day. Now it was spoiled.

The reports were still there on his desk, demanding his attention. The fly had disappeared, affronted perhaps at his defection.

It was half past seven. He dialed the number of his apartment on the Boulevard Richard-Lenoir.

"Is that you?"

It was what he always said. Absurd, really. As if he didn't recognize his wife's voice by now.

"Won't you be home for dinner?"

He so often wasn't that she took it for granted that this was what he was calling to say.

"As a matter of fact, I will. . . . What are we having? . . . Good. . . . Good. . . . In about half an hour."

He went into the duty room. Most of the inspectors had gone. He sat at Janvier's desk and scribbled a message on his pad, for him to telephone him at home as soon as he got back.

He was still feeling vaguely uneasy. There were a number of puzzling features about this case, and the fact that Florentin was, in some sense, an old friend didn't make things any easier.

And then there were the others, middle-aged men of some standing, each with a life of his own, regular habits, and a stable family background.

Except for one day a week! Except for those few furtive hours in Joséphine Papet's apartment.

Tomorrow the newspapers would be full of the story, and they would all shake in their shoes.

He ought to go up to the attic, to Criminal Records, and find out how Moers was getting on. With a shrug, he stood up and took his hat from its hook.

"See you tomorrow. . . ."

"Good night, Chief."

He fought his way through the evening crowds as far as the Châtelet, and there joined the queue waiting for his bus.

As soon as he came in, Madame Maigret could see that he had something on his mind, and he read the unspoken question in her glance.

"A wretched business!" he grumbled, as he went to the bathroom to wash his hands.

He took off his jacket and loosened his tie a little.

"I was at school with the fellow, and now he's up to his neck in this ghastly mess. . . . And frankly, I can't see anyone having the slightest sympathy for him in his predicament!"

"What is it, a murder?"

"A shooting. The woman is dead. . . ."

"What motive? Jealousy?"

"No, not if he did it."

"Is there any doubt about it?"

"Let's eat." He sighed, as though he had had more than enough of the subject.

All the windows were open, and the room was bathed in the golden light of the setting sun. There was chicken with tarragon, which Madame Maigret cooked to perfection, garnished with asparagus tips.

She had on a cotton housecoat printed all over with little flowers. It was one of several that she liked to wear at home. He felt tonight that it enhanced the domestic intimacy of their dinner together.

"Will you have to go out again?"

"I don't think so. I left a message for Janvier to phone me."

Just as he was digging his spoon into his half-melon, the telephone rang.

"Hello, yes. . . . Oh, it's you, Janvier. . . . Are you at the Quai? . . . Anything to report?"

"Very little, Chief. . . . First of all, I went into the two shops on the ground floor. . . . You remember, there's a lingerie shop on the left . . . Chez Éliane. . . . Very fancy stuff . . . the sort of thing you usually find only in Montmartre. . . . Apparently the tourists are crazy about it. . . .

"It's owned by two girls, one dark, one fair, and they seem to spend most of their time watching the comings and goings in the building. They had no difficulty in recognizing Florentin and the dead woman from my description. . . . She was a customer of theirs, though she didn't go in for any of the fancy stuff. . . .

"According to them, she was a charming woman, even-tempered, always ready with a smile. . . . Very much the little housewife . . . extremely neat in her person, and very kindhearted. . . .

"They knew about her and Florentin, and they thought a lot of him, too. . . . He struck them as quite the gentleman . . . a gentleman down on his luck was how they put it. . . .

"They saw Josée go out with the Wednesday visitor one

evening, but they didn't think any the worse of her for that. . . ."

"François Paré, do you mean? The Ministry of Public Works man?"

"I presume so. . . . Anyway, that's how they found out about his weekly visits. He always arrived in a black Citroën, punctual almost to the minute, except that he could never find anywhere to park. . . . And, invariably, he came around with a box of fancy cakes."

"Do they know about the other men, too?"

"Only the Thursday one. . . . He was the very first. . . . He's been coming to the Rue Notre-Dame-de-Lorette for years. . . . Some time in the distant past, they think, he actually lived in the apartment for several weeks. . . . They call him Fatty. . . . He has round pink cheeks, like a baby, and pale, protuberant eyes. . . .

"Almost every Thursday he took her out to dinner and the theater. . . . Ordinarily, he would have spent tonight in the apartment. . . . Quite often he didn't leave until lunchtime the following day."

Maigret consulted his notes.

"That would be Fernand Courcel, of Rouen. . . . He has an office in Paris, Boulevard Voltaire. . . . What about the others?"

"They didn't mention them, but they're convinced Florentin is the one she was deceiving."

"And what else?"

"Next, I went into the shoeshop opposite, Chaussures Martin. . . . It's a dark, narrow little place. You can't see into the street, because of the window display, though there is a glass door, if you should happen to be looking out. . . ."

"Go on. . . ."

"The apartment to the left on the first floor belongs to a dentist. He doesn't know a thing. Josée went to him for treatment about four years ago . . . a filling . . . she had three appointments. . . . On the right, there's an old couple who are practically housebound. The husband used to work for the Banque de France, I don't know in what capacity. They have one married daughter, who comes to see them every Sunday, with her husband and two children. . . .

"Then there's the apartment overlooking the courtyard. . . . It's empty at present. The tenants, a man and wife, have been in Italy for the past month. They're both in the catering business.

"On the second floor there's the woman who makes corsets. She has two girls working for her. . . . None of them had ever heard of Joséphine Papet.

"Across the way there's a woman with three children, all under five. . . . She's got a voice like a foghorn, and no wonder, considering the noise those kids make.

" 'It's disgusting,' she said. 'I've written to the landlord about it. My husband was against it, but I wrote all the same. . . . He's scared stiff of making trouble. . . . Carrying on like that in a respectable house, with children in it! . . . It was a different man almost every night. . . . I got to know which was which by the way they rang the bell. . . .

" 'The one with the limp always came on Saturdays, right after lunch. . . . You could tell him by his walk. . . . Besides, he always jabbed at the bell four or five times in quick succession. Poor fool, he probably thought he was the only one.' "

"Were you able to find out anything more about him?"

"Only that he's a man of about fifty, and always came by taxi."

"What about the redhead?"

"He's a new one. . . . He put in his first appearance only a few weeks ago. He's younger than the others, thirty or thirty-five, and it seems he takes the stairs four at a time. . . ."

"Has he got a key?"

"No, none of them had except Florentin. . . . According to my informant on the second floor, he's just a high-class pimp. . . .

" 'I'd rather have those you see around the Pigalle any day,' she said. 'They at least are taking a risk. . . . And anyway, they're not fit for any other sort of work. . . . But he looks as if he's seen better days, and seems to be a man of some education.' "

Maigret could not help smiling. He rather regretted not having interviewed the tenants himself.

"There was no answer from the apartment opposite, so I went up to the fourth floor, and there I walked straight into a family row.

"The husband was yelling at the top of his voice: 'If you don't tell me where you've been and who with . . .'

" 'Surely I've a perfect right to go out and do my shopping without having to give you a detailed account of every shop I've been into! What do you expect me to do, get a certificate from the manager wherever I go?'

" 'You don't expect me to believe you spent the whole afternoon buying a pair of shoes, do you? Who were you with? Answer me, will you!'

" 'I don't know what you're talking about.'

" 'You must have gone to meet someone. Who was it?'

"Frankly, I thought I'd better make myself scarce," commented Janvier.

"There's an old woman living opposite. It's amazing the number of old people there are in that district. She could tell me nothing. She's pretty deaf, and the apartment smells of stale food.

"As a last resort, I had a go at the concierge. . . . She just stared at me with those fish-eyes of hers, and I couldn't get a thing out of her."

"Nor could I, if that's any consolation. . . . Except that, according to her, no one went up to the apartment between three and four o'clock."

"Is she quite sure?"

"So she says. . . . She also says that she was in the lodge the whole time, and that no one could have gone past without her seeing them. . . . That's her story, and it's my belief she'll stick to it, even on oath."

"What shall I do next?"

"Go home. I'll see you tomorrow in the office."

"Good night, Chief."

Maigret, his melon still untasted, scarcely had time to put the receiver down when the telephone rang again. This time it was Lapointe. He seemed excited.

"I've been trying to get through to you for the last quarter of an hour, Chief, but the line was busy the whole time. Before that, I tried the Quai. . . . I'm speaking from the tobacconist's on the corner. . . . There have been developments, Chief. . . ."

"Go on."

"Before we were even out of the building, he knew he was being tailed. He actually turned around and winked at me as we were going down the stairs. . . .

"Outside, I followed about three or four yards behind him. When we got to the Place Dauphine, he seemed to hesitate, then he went toward the Brasserie Dauphine. . . . He looked at me as though he expected me to catch up with him, and when I didn't he came up and spoke to me.

" 'Look here, I'm going in for a drink. . . . I don't see any reason why you shouldn't join me, do you?'

"I had a feeling that he was making fun of me. He's a bit of a clown, isn't he? I said I didn't drink on duty, so he went in alone. I watched him gulp down three or four brandies, one after the other. . . . I'm not quite sure how many.

"When he came out, having made sure that I was still there, he gave me another wink and started off toward the Pont-Neuf. The streets were very crowded at that hour, and the cars were jammed bumper to bumper, with every other driver leaning on his horn. . . .

"We walked in single file as far as the Quai de la Mégisserie, and then suddenly he pulled himself up onto the parapet and jumped into the Seine! It all happened so quickly that only the few people nearest to him saw him do it.

"He came up within no more than a couple of yards of a boat made fast to the bank. By that time, quite a crowd had gathered. Then something almost comical happened. . . . The owner of the boat took hold of a long, heavy boat-hook and held it out to Florentin, who grabbed hold of the hook end and allowed himself to be hauled in like a fish!

"By the time I had scrambled down the bank and reached the boat, Florentin was on dry land, with a police constable bending over him.

"The whole place was swarming with spectators by then. . . . You'd have thought that something really serious had happened.

"I decided I'd better keep out of it, in case there were any reporters around who might be curious about what I was doing there. . . . So I kept watch from a distance. I hope I did the right thing. . . ."

"You did very well. . . . Besides, I can assure you that Florentin was never in any danger. . . . We used to go swimming together in the Allier as boys, and he was far and away the best swimmer in the school. What happened next?"

"The boatman gave him a glass of rum, not realizing that he'd already had three or four brandies, and then the policeman marched him off to the station at Les Halles.

"I didn't go in, for reasons I've already explained. I presume they took his name and address, and asked him a few questions. . . . When he came out, I was having a sandwich in the bistro opposite the police station, and I don't think he saw me. . . . He was a sorry sight, I must say, wrapped in an old police blanket they'd lent him. . . .

"He took a taxi back to his place. . . . He changed into dry clothes. . . . I could see him through the workshop window. . . . He caught sight of me as he came out, and treated me to another wink, and pulled a face at me for good measure. Then he walked as far as the Place Blanche, where he went into a restaurant. . . .

"He got back here half an hour ago, and bought a paper, and the last I saw of him he was stretched out on his bed, reading it."

By the time he had heard the whole story, Maigret was looking quite stunned.

"Did you have any dinner?"

"I had a sandwich. I see they sell sandwiches in here, so I'll probably have a couple more before I leave. . . . Torrence will be relieving me at two in the morning."

"Good luck to you," said Maigret, with a sigh.

"Shall I call you again if anything further happens?"

"Yes, no matter how late it is."

He had almost forgotten about his melon. It was dusk by now. He ate the melon over by the window, while Madame Maigret cleared the table.

One thing was certain. Florentin had had no intention of committing suicide. It is virtually impossible for a strong swimmer to drown in the Seine, especially in the middle of June, with the quays swarming with people, and within a few feet of a conveniently moored boat!

Why, then, had his old friend jumped into the water? To create the impression that he was being driven to distraction by the unfounded suspicions of the police?

"How is Lapointe?"

Maigret could not help smiling. He knew very well what his wife was getting at. She would never ask him point-blank about his work, but there were times when she was not above angling for information.

"He's in the best of health, which is just as well, because he's got several more hours ahead of him pounding the pavement at the end of a little alley off the Boulevard Roche-chouart."

"All on account of your old school friend?"

"Yes, he's just been making a spectacle of himself by jumping off the Pont-Neuf into the Seine."

"You mean he tried to commit suicide?"

"No, I'm quite sure he had no such intention."

What possible reason could Florentin have for drawing attention to himself in that way? Did he just want to get his name in the papers? Surely not, but then, where Florentin was concerned, anything was possible.

"Shall we go out for a breath of air?"

The street lights on the Boulevard Richard-Lenoir were all on, although it was not yet dark outside. They were not the only couple taking a quiet stroll, enjoying the cool of the evening after a hot day.

At eleven, they went to bed. Next morning, the sun was shining, promising another hot day. Already, a faint smell of tar rose from the streets, a smell characteristic of Paris in mid-summer, when the road surfaces seem almost to melt in the heat.

Maigret found a huge pile of mail waiting for him in his office, which all had to be dealt with before he could get down to his report. The morning papers mentioned the murder on the Rue Notre-Dame-de-Lorette, but they gave no details. Maigret reported to his Departmental Chief with a brief summary of the facts, as far as he knew them.

"Has he confessed?"

"No."

"Have you any real evidence against him?"

"Only pointers."

He saw no reason to add that he and Florentin had been at school together. As soon as he got back to his office, he sent for Janvier.

"One thing we know for certain: Joséphine Papet had four regular visitors. We have the names of two of them, François Paré and Courcel. I'll see them myself this morning. I'll leave the other two to you. Question as many people as you like, the neighbors, the tradesmen, anyone else you can think of, but I want their names and addresses before the day is out. . . ."

Janvier could not help smiling. Maigret knew as well as he did that it was an almost impossible assignment.

"I'm relying on you."

"Very good, Chief."

Next, Maigret telephoned the pathologist. Alas, it was no longer his dear old friend Doctor Paul, whose greatest pleasure in life had been to take him out to dinner and regale him, throughout the meal, with a detailed account of his autopsies.

"Have you recovered the bullet, Doctor?"

By way of reply, the doctor began reading from the report that he was in the middle of writing. Joséphine Papet had been in the prime of life and had enjoyed excellent health. All her organs were sound, and it was plain that she had been exceptionally fastidious in her personal habits.

As to the shot, it had been fired at a range of between eighteen inches and three feet.

"The bullet was on a slight upward trajectory when it lodged in the base of the skull."

Maigret could not help thinking of the tall figure of Florentin. Was it possible that he had fired the shot sitting down?

He put the question to the doctor.

"Could she have been shot by someone sitting down?"

"No, the angle of entry wasn't steep enough for that. A slight upward trajectory, I said. . . . I've sent the bullet to Gastinne-Renette for an expert opinion. . . . If you ask me, I don't believe that bullet was fired from an automatic weapon, but more probably from an old-fashioned cylinder revolver."

"Was death instantaneous?"

"Within half a minute at most, I'd say."

"So nothing could have been done to save her?"

"Absolutely nothing."

"Thank you, Doctor."

Torrence was back in the inspectors' room. He had been relieved by Dieudonné, who was new to the job.

"What's he been up to?"

"He got up at half past seven, shaved, had a quick wash, and went out in his slippers to the tobacconist's on the corner for breakfast. He had two cups of coffee, and two or three croissants. Afterward, he went into the phone booth. Presumably, he intended to make a call, but after some hesitation he came out without doing so.

"He turned around several times to see if I was watching. I don't know what he's like usually, but at the moment he seems listless and depressed. . . .

"He went to the newspaper stand on the Place Blanche and bought several papers. Then he just stood there in the street, glancing through a couple of them.

"After that, he went back indoors. . . . Then Dieudonné arrived and took over, and I came back here to report to you."

"Didn't he speak to anyone?"

"No. . . . Well, not unless you count the painter, who turned up while he was out buying the papers. I don't know where he lives, but he certainly doesn't sleep in his studio. . . . When Florentin got back, he called out: 'How goes it?'

"And the painter replied: 'Fine.' Then he gave me a dirty look. He must be wondering what on earth we're up to, keeping watch in relays at the head of the alley. He was still peering out, when Dieudonné took over from me."

Maigret took his hat off its hook and went out into the forecourt. Ordinarily, he would have taken an inspector with him, and driven off in one of the row of black cars parked in front of the building.

Today, however, he preferred to walk. He crossed the Pont Saint-Michel, making for the Boulevard Saint-Germain. He had never before had occasion to set foot in the Ministry of Public Works. He looked in bewilderment from one to another of the many staircases, each marked with a different letter of the alphabet.

"Can I help you?"

"I'm looking for the Department of Inland Waterways."

"Staircase C, top floor."

There was no elevator that he could see. The staircase was as dingy as his own at the Quai des Orfèvres. On each floor, black arrows were painted on the walls and pointed to the various offices along the corridor.

On the third floor, he found the sign he was looking for. He pushed open a door marked: *Enter without knocking.*

It led into a large room, where four men and two girls were working at desks, behind a balustrade.

The walls were covered with old, yellowing maps, just as in the classrooms of the lycée in Moulins.

"May I help you?"

"I'm looking for a Monsieur Paré."

"Your name, please?"

He hesitated. Very likely the Head of the Department of Inland Waterways was a man of impeccable character, and he had no wish to compromise him in the eyes of his staff. On reflection, he decided not to produce his card.

"My name is Maigret."

The youth, frowning, took a closer look at him, then, with a shrug, turned and disappeared through a door at the back of the room.

He was soon back.

"Monsieur Paré will see you now," he said, ushering Maigret into an inner room.

Maigret saw, coming forward to greet him, an elderly man of dignified bearing, though somewhat overweight. With formal ceremony, he invited Maigret to be seated.

"I was expecting you, Monsieur Maigret."

There was a morning paper lying on his desk. He lowered himself gently into the chair behind the desk, and laid his arms along the arms of the chair. There was a touch of ritual solemnity in the way he did this.

"I'm sure there is no need for me to tell you that, as far as I'm concerned, this is a very unpleasant situation."

He was not smiling. He had the air of a man who seldom smiled. He was self-possessed, a little pompous, the sort who would weigh his words carefully before speaking.

CHAPTER
THREE

The office was very much like the one Maigret had occupied before the Law Courts were modernized. There, on the mantelpiece, was a black marble clock identical with the one in his present office. Maigret wondered if it was as unreliable as his.

The man himself was as impassive as the clock. He was very much the senior civil servant, a combination of self-possession and caution. It must have been a deep affront to his self-esteem to find himself suddenly in a tough spot.

His features were undistinguished. His sparse brown hair was carefully combed to hide an incipient bald patch, and his little toothbrush mustache was too black to be natural. He had well-cared-for white hands, covered with long, fine hairs.

"It was good of you to come yourself, Monsieur Maigret, and spare me the indignity of a summons to Police Head-quarters."

"I'm as anxious as you are to avoid any unnecessary publicity."

"I noticed that the morning papers gave little more than the bare facts."

"Had you known Joséphine Papet long?"

"About three years. It gives me an odd feeling, you know, to hear you use her full name. . . . I've always known her as Josée. . . . As a matter of fact, it wasn't until several months after we met that I learned what her surname was. . . ."

"I understand. . . . How did you meet her?"

"It happened quite by chance. I'm fifty-five, Superintendent. I was fifty-two at the time, and it may surprise you to know I had never before been unfaithful to my wife.

"This, in spite of the fact that, for the past ten years, my wife has been a sick woman. She suffers from a psychiatric disorder, which has strained our relationship a good deal."

"Have you got any children?"

"Three daughters. The eldest is married to a shipowner in La Rochelle. The second is a schoolteacher in a lycée in Tunis. The youngest is also married. She lives in Paris, in the Sixteenth Arrondissement. I have five grandchildren in all; the oldest is nearly twelve. As to my wife and myself, we have lived in the same apartment in Versailles for thirty years. As you see, most of my life has been wholly uneventful, very much the life you would expect a conscientious civil servant to lead."

He spoke deliberately, choosing his words with care, as a prudent man should. There was not the faintest hint of self-mockery in his manner, and his face remained expressionless. Had he ever been known to burst out laughing? Maigret doubted it. Even his smile was probably no more than a twitch of the lips.

"You asked me where I met her. . . . Occasionally, when

I leave the office, I stop for a drink in a brasserie on the corner of the Boulevard Saint-Germain and the Rue de Solférino. . . . I did so on that day. . . . It was raining. . . . I can still see the rain streaming down the windows.

"I sat in my usual corner, and the waiter, who has known me for years, brought me my glass of port. . . .

"There was a young woman at the next table. She was writing a letter, and having trouble with the pen. She was using violet ink. There wasn't much left in the bottle, and what there was was reduced almost to a paste.

"She was a respectable-looking young woman, soberly dressed in a good navy blue suit. . . .

"She called out to the waiter: 'Is this the only pen you have?'

" 'I'm sorry, madam,' he said, 'but nowadays most of our customers use their own fountain pens.'

"I took mine from my pocket, and held it out to her. It was more or less a reflex action.

" 'Allow me,' I said.

"She took it, with a grateful smile. And that's how it all started. She had almost finished writing her letter. She was drinking tea.

"As she gave me back my pen, she asked: 'Do you come here often?'

" 'Almost every day,' I said.

" 'I like these old-fashioned brasseries, where most of the customers are regulars. They have atmosphere.'

" 'Do you live in this district?'

" 'No, I have an apartment on the Rue Notre-Dame-de-Lorette, but I'm quite often in this part of the world.' "

His expression, as he described this first meeting, was as artless as a child's.

"So you see, it was pure chance that we met. She wasn't there the following day, but the day after that she was back, sitting at the same table. She smiled at me.

"There was something about her, her manner, her expression, an air of gentle serenity. One felt one could trust her.

"We exchanged a few words. I told her I lived at Versailles, and I seem to remember that I mentioned my wife and daughters. She came to the door, and watched me get into my car and drive away.

"It may surprise you to know that things went on in this way for a month or more. Some days, she wasn't in the brasserie, and I always felt a pang of disappointment when I didn't see her. . . .

"I had come to look upon her as a friend, nothing more. It was just that, with my wife, I always had to weigh every word. She was so apt to take things amiss, and then there would be a scene. . . .

"Before my daughters left home, it was all very different. There were always noisy, cheerful young people about, and in those days my wife was energetic and high-spirited. You can't imagine what it's like to go home to a vast, empty apartment, and be watched from the minute you're in the door by a pair of eyes, full of anguish and mistrust. . . ."

Maigret, having lit his pipe, held out his tobacco pouch.

"No, thanks. I gave up smoking years ago. . . . Please don't imagine I'm making excuses for myself. . . .

"I am on the committee of a charitable organization that meets every Wednesday. . . . One Wednesday I skipped the meeting and went back with Mademoiselle Papet to her apartment. . . .

"By then she had told me quite a lot about herself, including the fact that she lived alone on a modest income inherited from her parents. She had repeatedly tried to get some sort of job, she said, but without success."

"Did she ever talk about her family?"

"Her father, who had been an officer in the regular army, was killed in the war when she was a child. . . . She lived in the provinces with her widowed mother until she grew up. . . . She had one brother."

"Did you ever see him?"

"Only once. He was an engineer, and he traveled a good deal. One Wednesday I arrived early, and he happened to be there, and she introduced us.

"He was distinguished-looking, a good deal older than she was. He's no fool. He recently patented a process for eliminating the toxic gases in exhaust fumes."

"Is he tall and thin, with light gray eyes and an unusually mobile face?"

François Paré looked surprised.

"Do you know him?"

"I've met him. Forgive me for asking, but did you give Josée much money?"

The Head of Inland Waterways flushed and averted his eyes.

"I'm in the fortunate position of being comfortably well off, more than comfortably well off. I was left two farms in Normandy by a brother of my mother's. I could have retired years ago, except that I shouldn't know what to do with myself if I did."

"Would it be fair to say that you were supporting her?"

"Not exactly. . . . I saw to it that she didn't have to watch every penny, and perhaps enabled her to enjoy a few small extra comforts. . . ."

"You only saw her once a week, on Wednesdays?"

"It was the only day I had an excuse for spending the evening in town. . . . My wife grows more jealous and possessive with every year that passes. . . ."

"I take it she doesn't go so far as to spy on your movements?"

"No. She hardly ever goes out. . . . She's so thin that she can scarcely stand up. . . . She's seen innumerable doctors, but they all say it's hopeless."

"Did Mademoiselle Papet lead you to believe that you were her only lover?"

"It's not a word either of us would ever have thought of using . . . although, in the sense that our relations were intimate—I won't deny that—I suppose we were lovers. . . .

"But that wasn't the real bond between us. It was more that we were both lonely people, trying to put a good face on things. . . . I don't quite know how to put it. . . . We talked the same language. . . . We were able to open our hearts to one another. . . . In other words, we were friends."

"Were you jealous?"

He started, then gave Maigret a hostile look, as though he resented the question.

"I have taken you into my confidence. I've told you that she was the first and only woman in my life, other than my wife. . . . You know that I'm not a young man. . . . I haven't attempted to hide the fact that I set very great store by our relationship. I looked forward with eager impatience to those Wednesdays. You might even say I lived for Wednesday evening. . . . It was our time together that made life endurable for me. . . ."

"In other words, you would have been shattered to learn that she had another lover?"

"Of course. . . . It would have been the end. . . ."

"The end of what?"

"Of everything. . . . Of the happiness I had known for the past three years . . . a modest enough share, in a lifetime. . . ."

"You say you met her brother only once?"

"Yes."

"And you didn't suspect anything?"

"What was there to suspect?"

"Did you never meet anyone else in the apartment?"

He gave a ghost of a smile.

"Just once, a few weeks ago. As I got out of the elevator I saw a youngish man leaving the apartment."

"A man with red hair?"

He stared at Maigret in amazement.

"How did you know? Well, anyway, if you know that, you must also know that he's an insurance salesman. I must confess I followed him, and saw him go into a bar on the Rue Fontaine. . . . I got the impression that he was a regular there. . . .

"When I asked Josée about him, she didn't seem in the least embarrassed.

"She just said: 'He keeps pestering me to take out a life-insurance policy. This is the third time he's called. But what use would such a policy be to me? I have no dependents. . . . I must have his card somewhere. . . .'

"And she began opening drawers and searching through them, and she did, in fact, find a visiting card in the name of Jean-Luc Bodard, of Continentale, with offices on the Avenue de l'Opéra. It's not one of the larger companies, but it has an excellent reputation. . . . I spoke to the personnel manager, and he confirmed that Jean-Luc Bodard was one of their agents."

Maigret was puffing reflectively at his pipe. He was playing for time, painfully aware of the distasteful task ahead.

"I take it you went to the apartment yesterday?"

"Yes, just as usual. . . . I was a little late. I had to see the Permanent Under-Secretary, and it took longer than I expected. . . . I rang the bell, and I was surprised to get no reply.' . . . I rang again, and then knocked, but there was still no answer. . . ."

"Did you speak to the concierge?"

"That woman frightens me. . . . I never go near her if I can help it. . . . I didn't go straight home. . . . I dined alone in a restaurant at the Porte de Versailles. Officially, I was supposed to be at my committee meeting. . . ."

"When did you first learn of the murder?"

"This morning, while I was shaving. . . . I was listening to the news on the radio. It was just a bare announcement, no details. . . . I didn't see it in the papers until after I got here. I'm absolutely shattered. . . . I can't understand it. . . ."

"You weren't there, by any chance, between three and four yesterday afternoon?"

He replied with some bitterness:

"I understand what you are getting at. . . . I never left the office yesterday afternoon. My staff will confirm that, though, naturally, I should much prefer to have my name kept out of it. . . ."

Poor man! He really was shattered, torn between grief and anxiety. His Indian summer, with all that it had meant to him, had come to a sudden and shocking end, yet he was still very much concerned to preserve his reputation.

"I realized that you were bound to find out about me from either the concierge or Josée's brother, if he's in Paris. . . ."

"There was no brother, Monsieur Paré."

He frowned, in angry disbelief.

"I'm terribly sorry to disillusion you, but you'd have to learn the truth some time. The real name of the man who was introduced to you as Léon Papet is Léon Florentin. . . . It's an odd coincidence, but he and I were schoolboys together at the lycée in Moulins."

"I don't understand. . . ."

"No sooner were you out of Joséphine Papet's apartment than he was letting himself in with his key. . . . Did she ever give you a key?"

"No. I never asked for one. It wouldn't have occurred to me. . . ."

"He practically lived in the apartment, but when visitors were expected he disappeared. . . ."

"Did you say visitors, in the plural?"

He was very pale, and sat rigid in his chair, as though turned to stone.

"There were four of you, not counting Florentin."

"What do you mean?"

"I mean that Joséphine Papet was being kept, more or less, by four separate admirers. . . . One of them she knew long before you met. . . . In fact, many years ago he practically lived in the apartment for a time. . . ."

"Have you seen him?"

"Not yet."

"Who is he?"

In spite of everything, François Paré still believed that there must be some mistake.

"His name is Fernand Courcel. He and his brother own a ball-bearing factory in Rouen, with head offices in Paris, Boulevard Voltaire. He's about your age, and a good deal overweight. . . ."

"I find it hard to believe."

"His day was Thursday. He was the only one privileged to spend the night in the apartment."

"This isn't a trap, by any chance?"

"How do you mean?"

"I don't know. One hears that the police sometimes resort to devious methods. All you've said seems so utterly incredible to me. . . ."

"There was also a Saturday visitor. I know very little about him, except that he has a limp. . . ."

"What about the fourth man?"

He was putting a brave face on it, but he was gripping the arms of his chair so tightly that his knuckles showed white.

"The insurance salesman whom you saw coming out of the apartment. He's generally known as the redhead, on account of his red hair."

"He is a real insurance salesman. I checked up on him myself."

"Being an insurance salesman doesn't stop a man from also being the lover of an attractive woman."

"I don't understand. . . . You never knew her. . . . If you had, you would have found it just as impossible to believe . . . I never met anyone like her. She was so sane, so serene, so unassuming. . . . I have three daughters, so I should know something about women. . . . I'd have trusted her with my life, more than any of my children. . . ."

"I'm sorry to have to disillusion you."

"I take it you're quite sure of your facts?"

"If you wish, I can arrange for Florentin to tell you himself."

"I absolutely refuse to meet that man, or, indeed, any of the others. If I understand you, Florentin was what is known as her 'steady'?"

"More or less. . . . He's tried his hand at most things, in

his time, and never succeeded at anything. . . . In spite of which, he has a kind of fascination for women. . . ."

"He's almost as old as I am."

"Yes, just a couple of years younger. But he has one great advantage over you. . . . He's available at all times of the day and night. . . . Besides, he's never serious about anything. He takes each day as it comes, and lives entirely according to the whim of the moment."

Paré was a very different case. He bore the burden of a conscience, a sense of guilt. He took life with deadly seriousness. It showed in every line of his face, in every gesture he made.

It was almost as though he were shouldering the whole responsibility for his department, if not for the entire Ministry. Maigret found it hard to imagine him in the company of a woman like Josée.

Fortunately for him, she had been of an equable disposition. No doubt she had been one of those women who could sit, smiling and nodding for hours at a stretch, while a man, embittered by misfortune, unburdened himself of all his misery.

Maigret was beginning to form a clearer picture of her. She was nothing if not practical, and she knew the value of money. She had bought herself a house in Montmartre, and she had had forty-eight thousand francs salted away. Very likely, given time, she would have acquired a second, and possibly a third house.

There are some women for whom houses are the only hard currency, as though nothing in life has any real substance but bricks and mortar.

"Did you never think that she might come to a tragic end, Monsieur Paré?"

"Never for an instant. . . . She seemed to me the very

embodiment of stability and security. Everything about her, her life, her home . . ."

"Did she tell you where she came from originally?"

"From Poitiers, if I remember rightly."

A wise precaution, telling each of them a different story.

"Did she strike you as a woman of some education?"

"She had her bachelor's degree, and she had worked for a time as secretary to a lawyer."

"Did she mention the name of the lawyer?"

"She may have. I don't remember."

"Had she never been married?"

"Not to my knowledge. . . ."

"Were you not surprised by her reading tastes?"

"She was sentimental, rather naïve, really. It's not surprising that she enjoyed romantic novels. But she was the first to laugh at her own foibles."

"I don't want to distress you more than is absolutely necessary, but there is one thing I must ask you. Think back. . . . Try to remember everything you can. . . . You never know: the most trivial detail, a few casual words, something that may seem to you of no importance, could provide us with a clue. . . ."

François Paré levered his heavy frame out of the chair. He seemed uncertain whether or not to offer his hand to Maigret.

"I really can't think of anything. . . ."

He hesitated, then, his voice suddenly toneless, asked:

"Did she suffer much, do you know?"

"According to the pathologist, death was instantaneous."

Maigret saw his lips move, presumably in silent prayer.

"Thank you. I very much appreciate your discretion in this matter. I'm only sorry we could not have met in happier circumstances."

"So am I, Monsieur Paré."

Phew! As soon as he was on the stairs Maigret took a deep breath. He felt as though he had just emerged from a tunnel, and was much in need of the fresh air of the daylight world.

Although his interview with the Head of Inland Waterways had not yielded any tangible results, or told him anything that could be immediately useful, it had enabled him to form a clearer picture of the young woman herself.

Had she entrapped all her patrons by means of a letter written with a faulty pen in a brasserie frequented by a prosperous class of customer, or had her meeting with Paré been truly accidental?

The first of her lovers, as far as was known, had been Fernand Courcel. She must have been twenty-five at that time. What had she been doing before that? Maigret could not imagine her, with that well-bred air of hers, loitering around the Madeleine or the Champs-Elysées.

Perhaps she really had been secretary to some lawyer or other?

There was a light breeze on the Boulevard Saint-Germain, causing a faint tremor among the leaves of the trees. Maigret savored the morning air as he walked along. Turning off into a little side street leading to the Quais, he noticed a bistro with a pleasantly old-fashioned air. There was a truck parked in front of it, from which crates of wine were being unloaded.

He went in and, resting his elbows on the zinc counter, asked:

"Where do you get your wine?"

"From Sancerre. I come from those parts myself, and I get my supplies from my brother-in-law."

"I'll have a glass."

It was dry yet at the same time fruity. The bar counter was made of good old-fashioned zinc, and there was sawdust on the red-tiled floor.

"Another, please."

Joséphine, it seemed, had been a purveyor of dreams. What a very odd calling! He had three more men to see, three more of her lovers.

François Paré would not find it easy to replace her. Who else would listen to the outpourings of his sad old heart? Florentin had been driven back to his workshop in Montmartre, to a miserable bed in a windowless cubbyhole.

Better get on to the next one! He sighed as he went out of the bistro and made his way toward the Quai des Orfèvres.

Another illusion to be destroyed, more dreams to be shattered!

When he had reached the top of the stairs, Maigret, making his way down the long corridor of the Law Courts, paused automatically to look into the glass-walled waiting room, always jocularly referred to by the inspectors as "the fish bowl."

Much to his surprise, he saw, sitting in two of the uncomfortable green velvet armchairs, Léon Florentin in company with a stranger, a smallish man, fat, with a round face and blue eyes, unmistakably one who appreciated the good things of life.

At present, however, he seemed distressed. Florentin was speaking to him in an undertone, and every now and then, as he listened, he dabbed his eyes with a handkerchief, which was crumpled into a ball in his hand.

Across the room, ignoring them, and absorbed in the racing page of a newspaper, was Inspector Dieudonné.

Maigret passed by unnoticed. As soon as he got to his office he rang the bell for old Joseph, who appeared almost at once.

"Has anyone been asking for me?"

"Two men, sir."

"Which of them got here first?"

"This one, sir."

He handed Florentin's card to Maigret.

"And the other one?"

"He arrived about ten minutes later. He seemed very up-set. . . ."

The stranger, it turned out, was Fernand Courcel, of the firm of Courcel Frères, manufacturers of ball bearings in Rouen. The card also gave an address on the Boulevard Voltaire.

"Which will you see first?"

"Bring in Monsieur Courcel."

He sat down at his desk, with a brief glance through the open window at the shimmering sunlight outside.

"Come in. . . . Please sit down."

The man was smaller and fatter than Maigret had expected him to be, but there was something attractive about him; he had an infectious vitality and unfeigned good nature.

"You don't know me, of course, Superintendent. . . ."

"If you had not come here this morning, Monsieur Courcel, I should have called on you in your office."

The blue eyes widened in surprise, but there was no hint of fear in them.

"You know?"

"I know that you and Mademoiselle Papet were very close friends, and that it must have been a terrible shock this morning when you heard the news on the radio or read it in the paper."

Courcel's face crumpled, as though he were about to burst into tears, but he managed to control himself.

"I'm sorry. . . . I'm absolutely shattered. . . . She was much more than a friend to me. . . ."

"I know."

"In that case, there isn't much I can tell you, because I've no idea what could possibly have happened. . . . She was the kindest, the most discreet woman. . . ."

"Do you know the man who was talking to you in the waiting room?"

It was hardly possible to imagine anyone less like a captain of industry. The owner of the ball-bearing factory stared at him in astonishment.

"Didn't you know she had a brother?"

"When did you first meet him?"

"About three years ago. . . . Soon after he got back from Uruguay."

"Had he been there long?"

"Haven't you interviewed him?"

"I'd like to hear what he told you."

"He's an architect. He was there on a government contract to build a new town."

"You met him in Joséphine Papet's apartment?"

"That's right."

"Did you, on that occasion, arrive unexpectedly early?"

"To tell you the truth, I don't remember."

He was taken aback by the question. He frowned, and Maigret noticed that his eyebrows, like his hair, were very fair, almost white. This coloring, combined with his delicate pink and white complexion, gave him the appearance of a chubby baby.

"I don't quite see what you're getting at."

"Did you ever see him again?"

"Three or four times. . . ."

"Always on the Rue Notre-Dame-de-Lorette?"

"No. He came to see me in my office. . . . He had a scheme for developing the coastline between Le-Grau-du-Roi and Palavas as a luxury seaside resort, with hotels, houses and bungalows, and so on. . . ."

"And he thought he might interest you in the project?"

"That's right. . . . There was a lot to be said for it, I must admit. . . . I don't doubt that it will be a success. Unfortunately, I have no capital of my own. My brother and I own the business jointly, and I can't act independently of him. . . ."

"So you weren't able to help him at all?"

He flushed, much taken aback by Maigret's manner.

"I lent him a few thousand francs, just to enable him to register the plans."

"Do you know if the plans were, in fact, registered? Did he send you copies?"

"As I told you, I wasn't interested."

"Was that the only time he touched you for a loan?"

"I don't care for your way of putting it, but no. . . . He came to see me again last year. . . . It's always the same with any far-reaching project. . . . There are bound to be problems and difficulties. His office in Montpellier . . ."

"Is that where he lives?"

"Yes, didn't you know?"

They were at cross-purposes, and Fernand Courcel was beginning to show signs of impatience.

"Look here, why not have him in and ask him yourself?"

"His turn is coming."

"You seem to have it in for him, for some reason."

"Not at all, Monsieur Courcel. . . . In fact, I may as well tell you that he's an old school friend of mine. . . ."

The little man took a gold cigarette case out of his pocket and opened it.

"May I smoke?"

"Please do. How many times did you lend him money?"

He thought for a moment, then said:

"Three times. The last time, he had left his checkbook at home. . . ."

"What was he saying to you, out there in the waiting room?"

"Must I answer that?"

"It would be best."

"It's such a painful subject. . . . Oh, well!"

He sighed, stretched out his little legs, and drew deeply on his cigarette.

"He is entirely in the dark as to his sister's finances. . . . So am I, as it happens, but then it's no business of mine. He's invested every penny he owns in this project of his, so, naturally, he's short of ready cash for the time being. . . . He asked me to contribute to the funeral expenses. . . ."

Maigret smiled broadly. This really was too much! Courcel was outraged.

"Forgive me. You'll soon see why I can't help smiling. First of all, I'm bound to tell you that the real name of the man you know as Léon Papet is Léon Florentin. His father was a baker in Moulins, and he and I were at school together at the Lycée Banville."

"You mean he isn't her brother?"

"No, my dear sir, he is not. He is not her brother, nor even her cousin, but that doesn't alter the fact that he was living with her. . . ."

"You mean . . ."

He had sprung to his feet, as though stung.

"No!" he exclaimed. "It's not possible. Josée was incapable . . ."

He was pacing up and down the room, dropping his ash on the carpet.

"You must remember, Superintendent, that I have known her for ten years. . . . In the early days, before I was married, we lived together. . . . It was I who found the apartment on the Rue Notre-Dame-de-Lorette, and I spent a great deal of time and care decorating and furnishing it to suit her tastes."

"She was about twenty-five at that time, wasn't she?"

"Yes, and I was thirty-two. My father was still alive then, and my brother Gaston was running the office in Paris. So I was left with a good deal of time on my hands. . . ."

"Where and how did you meet?"

"I knew you'd ask me that, and I realize how it must look to you. . . . I met her in a night club in Montmartre, the Nouvel Adam. . . . It's not there any more. . . ."

"Did she just take her turn with the other girls?"

"No, she was a hostess, so she didn't have to entertain just anyone, only if she was specifically asked for. . . . I found her sitting alone at a table. . . . She was wearing a very simple black dress, and almost no make-up. . . . She looked sad, I thought, and rather shy, so much so that I hesitated for a long time before going up to speak to her."

"Did you spend the whole evening with her?"

"Naturally. . . . She told me all about her childhood. . . ."

"Where did she say she grew up?"

"La Rochelle. . . . Her father was a fisherman. He was drowned at sea. . . . She had four younger brothers and sisters. . . ."

"And her mother? Dead too, I wager. . . ."

Courcel glared at him furiously.

"Do you wish me to go on? If so . . ."

"Do forgive me. . . . But, you see, it's all a pack of lies."

"You mean she didn't have four brothers and sisters?"

"No, and it wasn't in order to bring them up that she was working in a cabaret in Montmartre. That was her story, wasn't it?"

He returned to his chair and sat, staring at the floor. Then, after some hesitation, he said:

"I find it hard to believe. . . . I was passionately in love with her."

"And yet you got married."

"Yes, I married a cousin. . . . I felt the years were slipping by, and I wanted children."

"You live in Rouen?"

"Most of the week, yes."

"But not Thursdays."

"How do you know?"

"On Thursdays you took Josée out to dinner and then to a theater or the movies, and spent the night in the apartment on the Rue Notre-Dame-de-Lorette."

"That's right. . . . When I married, I intended to break it off, but I found I couldn't."

"Did your wife know?"

"Of course not!"

"What about your brother?"

"I had to take Gaston into my confidence. . . . Supposedly, you see, I paid a weekly visit to our Marseilles office. . . ."

With quite touching candor, the little man added:

"He says I'm an idiot. . . ."

Maigret just managed to suppress a smile.

"When I think that only a few minutes ago I almost burst into tears when that man . . ."

"Florentin wasn't the only one. . . ."

"What are you insinuating?"

"I give you my word, Monsieur Courcel, that if she had died in any other way I would have spared you this. But she was murdered. It is my duty to find the man who killed her, and that can't be done without bringing the truth out into the open."

"Do you know who shot her?"

"Not yet. There were three men, besides yourself and Florentin, who visited her regularly."

He shook his head, as though even now he could not believe it.

"There were times when I almost made up my mind to marry her. If it hadn't been for Gaston, it's more than likely that . . ."

"Wednesday was the day of a senior civil servant. . . . He didn't spend the night in the apartment. . . ."

"Have you seen him?"

"This morning."

"Did he admit it?"

"He was perfectly open about his visits, and the nature of his relationship with Josée."

"How old is he?"

"Fifty-five. Did you ever see a man with a limp, if not in the apartment, then perhaps in the elevator?"

"No."

"There was a man with a limp, a middle-aged man. I'll find him soon enough, if one of my men hasn't done so already. . . ."

"Who else?" He sighed, clearly feeling that the sooner he knew the worst, the better.

"A man with red hair, a good deal younger than the rest of you. He's not much over thirty, and he's an insurance salesman."

"I take it you never knew her when she was alive?"

"That is so."

"If you had, you'd understand how I feel. You'd have thought she was as honest as the day is long, so frank and open as to be almost childlike. . . . I could have sworn . . ."

"Were you supporting her?"

"It was a hard job to persuade her to take a penny. . . .

She wanted to work in a shop, selling lingerie or something of the sort. . . . But she wasn't strong. . . . She was subject to spells of giddiness. She was always reproaching me for being too generous. . . ."

He was suddenly struck by a thought that had not, up to then, occurred to him.

"What about the others? Did they . . ."

"I'm afraid so, Monsieur Courcel. . . . Three of you, at least, were keeping her. I don't know about the redhead yet, but it won't be long before I do. The civil servant whom I saw this morning, at any rate, certainly was. . . ."

"But what did she do with the money? She had such simple tastes. . . ."

"She began by buying a house on the Rue du Mont-Cenis. And furthermore, after her death, forty-eight thousand francs in cash were found in the apartment. . . . Now, I must ask you to try to get hold of yourself and think back. . . . I won't ask you where you were between three and four yesterday afternoon. . . ."

"I was in my car on the way from Rouen. I drove through the Saint-Cloud tunnel, and I must have come out the other end at about a quarter past three. . . ."

He pulled himself up sharply, and stared at Maigret in blank astonishment.

"You can't mean you suspect me!"

"I don't suspect anyone. It's a purely routine question. . . . What time did you get to your office?"

"I didn't go straight there. I stopped off for a minute or two at a bar on the Rue de Ponthieu, to place a bet on a horse. . . . I go there regularly. . . . It wasn't, in fact, until about a quarter past five that I got to the Boulevard Voltaire. . . . Nominally, my brother and I are partners. . . . I spend a couple of days a week at the factory, and I have an office and a secretary on the Boulevard Voltaire, but in practice they could manage perfectly well without me. . . ."

"Does your brother not resent having to carry such a large share of the burden?"

"Quite the contrary. The less I do, the happier he is. . . . That way, he's the boss, don't you see?"

"What make is your car, Monsieur Courcel?"

"A Jaguar convertible. . . . I've always had a convertible. . . . My present one is pale blue. . . . Do you want the number?"

"That won't be necessary."

"When I think that not only Josée but her so-called brother . . . what did you say his name was?"

"Florentin. His father made the best cakes in Moulins."

He clenched his little fists.

"Don't distress yourself. Unless events take an unexpected turn, your name will be kept out of it. You may rest assured that I will treat all you have said in the strictest confidence. . . . Is your wife jealous?"

"I daresay she is, in a mild way. She suspects me of kicking over the traces once in a while, in Marseilles or Paris. . . ."

"Has there ever been anyone, apart from Josée?"

"Occasionally. . . . I suppose, like most other men, I'm curious about the unknown."

He looked about him for his hat, then remembered that he had left it in the waiting room. Maigret went with him, fearing that he might be tempted to attack Florentin.

Florentin looked at them glumly, obviously in some trepidation as to what Courcel's reaction would be.

When the little captain of industry had gone, Inspector Dieudonné, who had stood up when Maigret came into the waiting room, asked:

"Shall I report to you now, Chief?"

"Has something happened?"

"No. After he'd had breakfast in the bistro on the corner, he went back to his room and stayed there till nine thirty, when he left to come here by métro. He asked to see you. Soon after, the other gentleman arrived. They shook hands and talked. I didn't hear what they said. . . ."

"Thanks. That will be all for today."

Maigret motioned to Florentin.

"Come with me."

He ushered him into his office, shut the door, and gazed at him reflectively for a considerable time. Florentin, meanwhile, kept his eyes resolutely lowered, and his long bony frame, slumped in a chair, was limp, seeming almost on the point of collapsing.

"You're even a worse scoundrel than I thought."

"I know."

"What possessed you to do a thing like that?"

"I'd no idea I should run into him here. . . ."

"What have you come here for?"

He raised his head and gave Maigret an anguished look.

"Guess how much money I have in my pocket."

"What's that got to do with it?"

"I assure you, it has everything to do with it. All I have left in the world is a fifty-centime piece. . . . There isn't a shop or restaurant or café in the neighborhood willing to give me credit. . . ."

This time it was the Chief Superintendent who looked staggered, just as his fat little visitor had done a short while before.

"Have you come here to ask me for money?"

"Who else can I turn to, in my present fix? I don't doubt you told that pompous ass Paré that I'm not really Josée's brother. . . ."

"Naturally."

"So you robbed him of all his illusions, did you? I bet it shook him!"

"Be that as it may, he has a cast-iron alibi. Yesterday, between three and four, he was in his office."

"And to think that when I saw that little runt coming into the waiting room, I thought to myself that there was still hope for me!"

"The funeral expenses! Aren't you ashamed of yourself?"

Florentin shrugged.

"When one has had cause to be ashamed as often as I have . . . Mind you, I guessed he'd tell you about it. . . . But, as I got here first, there was just a chance that you might hear my story before he got his oar in. . . ."

Maigret stood up and went over to the window. He drank in the fresh air as though it were nectar. Florentin watched him in silence.

"What will happen to the forty-eight thousand francs?"

Maigret gave a violent start. It really was almost inconceivable that, at a time like this, Florentin should still be thinking about Josée's money.

"Can't you understand that I'm absolutely destitute? Look, there's no point in trying to deceive you. . . . It's true, I do occasionally sell a piece of furniture for a few hundred francs, but the antique business was only a front. . . ."

"I realized that."

"Well, then, just until I get on my feet . . ."

"What do you intend to do?"

"If necessary, I'll sign on as a porter in Les Halles."

"I must warn you that you won't be able to leave Paris."

"So I'm still under suspicion?"

"Until we get the man who did it. . . . Do you really know nothing of the man with the limp?"

"Even Josée didn't know his surname. . . . She called him Victor. . . . He never mentioned a wife or children. . . . She had no idea what he did for a living. . . . He was prosperous-looking. He wore good suits and custom-made shirts. . . . Oh, and there's one other thing I've just remembered. Once, she told me, when he took out his wallet, she saw his railroad season ticket. It was a Paris-Bordeaux ticket. . . ."

Here, at least, was something for his men to work on. Surely, there could not be many Paris-Bordeaux season tickets?

"I'm doing my best to be helpful, you see. . . ."

Maigret, taking the hint, got out his own wallet and extracted a hundred-franc note.

"You'd better make it last."

"Are you going on keeping me followed?"

"Yes."

He opened the door to the inspectors' room.

"Leroy."

He gave the necessary instructions and, this time, could see no way of avoiding shaking the hand of his old school friend when it was held out to him.

CHAPTER
FOUR

It was three o'clock, and Maigret was standing at the open window, hands in his pockets, pipe clenched between his teeth, in an attitude familiar to all who knew him.

The sun was shining, the sky was a cloudless blue dome, yet it was raining in diagonal streaks, and the large, widely spaced raindrops formed black patches on the ground where they fell.

The door opened behind him.

"Come in, Lucas," he said, without looking around.

He had sent him up to the attic of the Law Courts to find out from Records whether Florentin had any previous convictions.

"Three convictions, Chief. Nothing very serious."

"Fraud?"

"The first conviction—that was twenty-two years ago—was for giving a rubber check. At that time he was living in a furnished apartment on the Avenue de Wagram. He was a fruit importer in those days, and he had an office on the

Champs-Elysées. He got a suspended sentence of six months.

"Eight years later he was convicted on charges of fraud and misappropriation. By then, he had moved to a small hotel in Montparnasse. This time he had to serve his prison sentence. . . .

"Five years ago, another rubber check. . . . Described as being of no permanent address. . . ."

"Thanks."

"Is there anything else I can do?"

"You'd better go to the Rue Notre-Dame-de-Lorette and have a word with the shopkeepers. Janvier has already taken statements from them, but I want you to ask them a specific question. I want to know whether any of them saw a light blue Jaguar convertible parked outside the building or in a nearby street between three and four yesterday afternoon. You'd better ask at the local garages as well."

Left to himself, he stood looking out of the window, frowning. Moers's men had failed to come up with anything of interest. Joséphine Papet's fingerprints were all over the apartment, which was only to be expected.

There were, however, no prints on any of the door handles. They had all been carefully wiped off.

Florentin's prints, too, were everywhere, including the clothes closet and the bathroom, but there were none on the drawer of the bedside table, which the murderer must have opened to get at the revolver.

The Chief Superintendent had been struck, from the first, by the scrupulous cleanliness of the flat. Joséphine Papet had neither maid nor cleaning woman. He could imagine her in the mornings, with a scarf tied around her head and the radio playing softly, going from room to room, dusting and cleaning with meticulous thoroughness.

He was wearing his most surly expression, which meant that he was dissatisfied with himself. The truth was that he had an uneasy conscience.

If he and Florentin had not been schoolboys together in Moulins, would he not, by now, have applied to the Examining Magistrate for a warrant for his arrest?

It was not that he and the baker's son had ever been close friends, exactly. Even in their school days, Maigret had had reservations about him.

Florentin had always been good for a laugh, and he had often risked punishment just for the sake of a bit of fun.

But had there not been a touch of defiance, even aggressiveness, in his attitude?

He didn't give a damn for anyone, and would mimic the tics and mannerisms of the teachers with cruel accuracy.

He had had a ready wit, but he was quick to take offense if one of his quips failed to raise a laugh.

Had he not, even then, been an outsider? Had he not begun to see himself as, in some sense, set apart? That was, perhaps, the reason why his sense of humor often gave offense.

As a grown man he had come to Paris, where he had alternated between periods of semirespectability and darker phases, during one of which he served a prison sentence.

But he had never admitted defeat. He still had an air about him, a kind of innate elegance, even in a threadbare suit.

He was a born liar, scarcely aware that he was lying. He always had told lies, and never seemed disconcerted when he was found out. It was as though he were saying:

"Well, it was a good story, anyway! Too bad it didn't work."

No doubt he had, in his time, haunted Fouquet's and other smart bars on the Champs-Elysées, not to mention cabarets and night clubs. Such places give a man a false sense of well-being.

Fundamentally, Maigret suspected, he was insecure. His clowning was, in reality, just a defense mechanism, a mask, behind which was concealed a sadly inadequate personality.

He was a failure, typical of his kind, and, what was worse and more painful, an aging failure.

Was it pity that was preventing Maigret from arresting him? Or was it rather that he simply could not believe that anyone as sharp as Florentin would, had he actually been guilty, have left so many clues pointing to himself?"

Take the matter of Josée's savings, for instance. He had removed the biscuit box to his own workshop, wrapped in that day's newspaper. Surely, he could have found a safer hiding place than the miserable hovel on the Boulevard Rochechouart, where, as he must have known, the police could not fail to search?

Then there was that lapse of time after the shot, when he had stayed hidden in the clothes closet. A whole quarter of an hour!

Was it fear that had kept him there, fear of meeting the murderer face to face?

And why had he chosen to go straight to Maigret, when the obvious course was to report to the local police?

There was certainly a strong enough case to justify Maigret in arresting him. Even the recent appearance on the scene of the young man known as the redhead told against him, for here surely was a real threat to Florentin's security, a younger man who might well succeed in ousting him from the cushy spot on which he depended for his very life.

Janvier knocked at the door, came in without waiting for an answer, and collapsed into a chair.

"We've got him at last, Chief!"

"The man with a limp?"

"Yes. . . . I've lost count of the number of phone calls I've made, including half a dozen to Bordeaux. I almost had to go on my knees to the Railroads to get them to give me a list of season-ticket holders. . . ."

He stretched out his legs and lit a cigarette.

"I hope to heaven I've got the right man! I don't know whether I've done the right thing, but I've asked him to come and see you. . . . He'll be here in about a quarter of an hour. . . ."

"I'd rather have seen him on his own ground."

"He lives in Bordeaux. When he's in Paris he has a suite in the Hôtel Scribe. It's almost next door to his office on the Rue Auber."

"Who is he?"

"If my information is correct, he's a man of some standing in Bordeaux. He has a house on the river in Les Chartrons, which is where all the old, established families live. As you'd expect, he's a winegrower in a big way, exporting mainly to Germany and the Scandinavian countries. . . ."

"Have you seen him?"

"I've spoken to him on the telephone."

"Did he seem surprised?"

"He was very snooty at first and asked me if this was some kind of joke. When I assured him that I really was from the C.I.D., he said he couldn't imagine what business the police could possibly have with him, and that we'd better keep out of his hair if we didn't want trouble. . . . So I told him it had to do with what had happened on the Rue Notre-Dame-de-Lorette."

"How did he take it?"

"There was a long silence, then he said:

" 'When does Chief Superintendent Maigret want to see me?'

" 'As soon as possible.'

" 'I'll come to the Quai des Orfèvres as soon as I've been through my mail.'

"His name is Lamotte," Janvier added, "Victor Lamotte. . . . If you'd like, I'll call the C.I.D. in Bordeaux while he's with you, and see if there's anything more they can tell me."

"Good man."

"You don't seem too happy. . . ."

Maigret shrugged. Wasn't it always this way, at this stage of an inquiry, before the case had really begun to take shape? After all, Florentin apart, he had never even heard of any of these people until yesterday.

This morning he had interviewed a chubby little man who, though eccentric, had not struck him as being a person of much character. If Courcel had not had the good fortune to be born the son of an industrialist, what would have become of him? Probably he would have been a traveling salesman, but there was really no telling. He might have ended up like Florentin, part parasite, part crook.

Joseph announced the visitor and ushered him in. The man, as expected, had a pronounced limp. To Maigret's surprise, he had snow-white hair and a flaccid face. He looked sixty.

"Come in, Monsieur Lamotte. . . . I'm sorry to have put you to the trouble of coming here. . . . I hope you had no difficulty in parking your car in the forecourt?"

"I leave all that to my chauffeur."

Naturally! He would have a chauffeur and, no doubt, in Bordeaux, a whole retinue of servants.

"I presume you know what I want to see you about?"

"The inspector mentioned the Rue Notre-Dame-de-Lorette. I couldn't quite make out what he was getting at."

Maigret was seated at his desk, filling his pipe. His visitor sat opposite him, facing the window.

"You know Joséphine Papet. . . ."

The man hesitated for a considerable time before replying.

"How did you find out?"

"As you are no doubt aware, we have our methods and sources of information. If we didn't, the prisons of this country would be standing empty."

"I don't quite see the relevance of that last remark. You're surely not insinuating . . ."

"I'm not insinuating anything. Have you seen a newspaper this morning?"

"Certainly. I read the papers, like anyone else."

"Then you must be aware that Joséphine Papet, commonly known as Josée, was murdered in her apartment yesterday afternoon. Where were you at that time?"

"Not on the Rue Notre-Dame-de-Lorette, at any rate."

"Were you at your office?"

"At what time?"

"Let's say between three and four."

"I was taking a walk on the Grands Boulevards."

"Alone?"

"What's so strange about that?"

"Do you often go for solitary walks?"

"Regularly, when I'm in Paris, for an hour in the morning, from ten to eleven or thereabouts, and again for an hour in the afternoon. My doctor will tell you that he has urged me to take regular exercise. Until recently I was a good deal overweight, and it was putting a strain on my heart."

"You realize, don't you, that that leaves you without an alibi?"

"Do I need one?"

"As one of Josée's lovers, yes."

If this was news to him, he showed no sign of it. Looking perfectly composed, he asked:

"Were there many of us?"

There was a tinge of irony in his voice.

"Four, to my knowledge, not counting the man who lived with her."

"So she had a man living with her, did she?"

"If my information is correct, your day was Saturday. I may say that each of the others had a specific day too."

"I'm a creature of habit. I lead a very regular life. Every Saturday, after my visit to the Rue Notre-Dame-de-Lorette, I catch the Bordeaux express, which gets me home well before bedtime."

"Are you married, Monsieur Lamotte?"

"Yes, married and with a family. One of my sons is in the business with me. He's in charge of our warehouse in Bordeaux. . . . Another represents the firm in Bonn and travels a good deal in the north. . . . My daughter and son-in-law live in London, with their two children. . . ."

"How long have you known Joséphine Papet?"

"Four years, or thereabouts."

"What did she mean to you?"

Condescendingly, not without a hint of contempt, he replied:

"She provided relaxation."

"In other words, you had no real affection for her?"

"Affection would be rather too strong a word."

"Perhaps I should say liking."

"She was a pleasant companion, and I believed her to be discreet. So much so that it surprised me that you were able to track me down. . . . May I ask who put you on to me?"

"To begin with, all we knew about you was that you called on Saturdays, and that you had a limp."

"A riding accident, when I was seventeen. . . ."

"You have a railway season ticket. . . ."

"Ah! I see. . . . Find the limping man with the Paris-Bordeaux season ticket!"

"There's one thing that puzzles me, Monsieur Lamotte. Staying at the Hôtel Scribe as you do, you are surrounded by bars where you could meet any number of attractive women of easy virtue. . . ."

The man from Bordeaux, determined not to be ruffled, answered equably, though not without a touch of condescension. After all, Les Chartrons, where he lived, was the Faubourg Saint-Germain of Bordeaux, the domain of ancient and noble families.

As far as Lamotte was concerned, Maigret was a policeman like any other. Policemen, of course, were necessary to protect the rights and property of honest citizens, but this was the first time he had ever come into direct contact with this class of person.

"What did you say your name was?"

"It's of no importance, but, if you must know, it's Maigret."

"To begin with, Monsieur Maigret, I am a man of regular habits. I was brought up to believe in certain principles which are, perhaps, scarcely fashionable nowadays. I am not in the habit of frequenting bars. It may seem strange to you, but I have not set foot in a bar or café in Bordeaux since my student days.

"As to receiving a woman of the sort you have in mind in my suite at the Scribe, you surely must see that it would scarcely be the thing, and besides, it would be risky. . . ."

"Blackmail, do you mean?"

"For a man in my position, there is always the risk. . . ."

"Yet you visited Josée once a week on the Rue Notre-Dame-de-Lorette?"

"A much less risky arrangement. You can understand that, surely?"

Maigret's patience was wearing thin.

"All the same, you must admit you knew precious little about her."

"What do you expect? Or perhaps you think I should have asked you to make inquiries on my behalf?"

"Where did you first meet her?"

"In the dining car."

"Was she going to Bordeaux?"

"No, she was returning to Paris. . . . We happened to be sitting opposite one another at a table for two. . . . She seemed a very respectable sort of woman. . . . When I passed her the breadbasket, I remember, she looked at me as though I had taken a liberty. . . . Later it turned out that we had seats in the same compartment."

"Did you have a mistress at that time?"

"Don't you think that's rather an impertinent question? Anyway, I can't see what it can possibly have to do with your present inquiries."

"You don't have to answer if you would rather not."

"I have nothing to hide. . . . I did have a mistress, a former secretary. I had set her up in an apartment on the Avenue de la Grande Armée. Just a week before I met Josée, she announced that she was going to be married."

"In other words, there was a vacancy to be filled. . . ."

"I don't care for your tone, and I'm not sure that I feel inclined to answer any more questions."

"In that case, I may have to detain you longer than you may find convenient."

"Is that a threat?"

"Just a warning."

"I'd be within my rights in refusing to answer questions

except in the presence of my lawyer, but it hardly seems worth the trouble. Let us continue."

He was now very much on his dignity.

"How long had you known Josée when you first went to the Rue Notre-Dame-de-Lorette?"

"About three weeks, perhaps a month. . . ."

"Did she say she had a job?"

"No."

"Did she claim to have independent means?"

"A modest allowance from one of her uncles."

"Did she tell you where she came from, originally?"

"Somewhere near Grenoble."

Joséphine Papet, it seemed, had been, like Florentin, a compulsive liar. She had invented a different family background for each of her lovers.

"Did you make her a generous allowance?"

"That's a most indelicate question!"

"Nevertheless, I should be glad if you would answer it."

"I gave her two thousand francs a month in an envelope, or I should say, rather, I left it discreetly on the mantelpiece."

Maigret smiled. It took him right back to his very early days on the Force, when there were still to be seen, about the Boulevards, elderly gentlemen in patent-leather shoes and white spats, ogling the pretty women through their monocles.

Those were the days of furnished mezzanine apartments and kept women, women not unlike Joséphine Papet, good-natured, warmhearted, discreet.

Victor Lamotte had not fallen in love. His life was centered on his family in Bordeaux. He was at home, not on the Rue Notre-Dame-de-Lorette, but in his austere family mansion, from which he ventured forth once or twice a week, to stay at the Hôtel Scribe and go to his office on the Rue Auber.

Nevertheless, he too had felt the need of a refuge, where he could drop the oppressive mask of respectability and open his heart to a woman. And was not Josée just the woman with whom a man could safely relax, without fear of unpleasant repercussions?

"Did you know any of her other 'protectors'?"

"You would hardly expect her to introduce us!"

"There might have been an accidental encounter. You could have come face to face with one of them leaving the apartment, say."

"As it happens, I didn't."

"Did you ever take her out?"

"No."

"What about your chauffeur? Did he wait outside?"

He shrugged. Evidently he thought Maigret somewhat naïve.

"I always took a taxi."

"Did you know she'd bought a house in Montmartre?"

"It's the first I've heard of it."

He was at no pains to conceal his total lack of interest in her personal affairs.

"What's more, forty-eight thousand francs in notes were found in her apartment."

"I daresay some of it was mine, but don't worry, I shan't ask for it back."

"Were you distressed to learn of her death?"

"To be honest with you, no. Millions of people die every day. . . ."

Maigret stood up. He had had enough. If this interview were to go on any longer, he would be hard put to it to conceal his disgust.

"Don't you want a signed statement from me?"

"No."

"Am I to expect a summons from the Examining Magistrate?"

"I can't answer that, at present."

"If it should come to a trial . . ."

"It will."

"Always supposing you get the murderer."

"We'll get him."

"I'd better warn you that I shall take steps to keep my name out of it. I have influential friends. . . ."

"I don't doubt it."

Whereupon the Chief Superintendent stepped over to the door and held it wide open. As he was going out, Lamotte turned back as though intending to say something by way of leave-taking, but then, apparently thinking better of it, went off without a word.

That was three of them dealt with. There still remained the redhead. Maigret was in a foul temper, and felt he must give himself a little time to cool off. He went back to his desk and sat down. It had stopped raining some time ago. A fly—perhaps the same one that had haunted him the previous day—flew in through the window and settled on the sheet of paper on which he was idly doodling.

Abruptly, he woke up to the fact that his wandering pencil had formed a word:

Premeditation.

Unless Florentin had done it, premeditation seemed unlikely. The killer had come to the apartment unarmed. Undoubtedly, he was a familiar visitor, since he knew that there was a revolver in the bedside table drawer.

Was it not possible that he had intended all along to make use of it?

Assuming, for the sake of argument, that Florentin really had been hiding in the clothes closet, and was telling the truth, what reason could the intruder have had for hanging about in the bedroom for a full quarter of an hour, especially in view of the fact that, as he moved about the room, he would have had to step back and forth across the body repeatedly?

Had he been searching for the money? If so, why had he not found it, since all he would have had to do was force a very flimsy lock?

Letters? A document of some sort?

Which of them needed money? Not François Paré, the civil servant, nor tubby little Fernand Courcel. Still less the high and mighty Victor Lamotte.

Any one of them, on the other hand, might well have reacted violently to attempted blackmail.

As usual, he had got back to Florentin—Florentin, whom the Examining Magistrate would certainly have ordered Maigret to arrest, had he been fully informed of the facts.

Maigret had hoped that an opportunity to question Jean-Luc Bodard, known as the redhead, would not be long delayed, but the inspector who had been sent to find him returned with a disappointing report.

The young insurance agent was out on his rounds and he was not expected back till the evening.

He lived in a small hotel, the Hôtel Beauséjour, on the Boulevard des Batignolles, and took his meals in the restaurant.

Maigret was fretful, as always when he felt that something was amiss with the case he was working on. He was uneasy and dissatisfied with himself. He could not bring himself to settle down to the paperwork cluttering up his desk. He got up, went across to the door leading to the inspectors' duty room, and opened it.

"Lapointe," he called. "Come along. I need a car."

It was not until they were driving along the Quai that he said grumpily: "Rue Notre-Dame-de-Lorette."

He had the feeling that he had overlooked something important. It was as though the truth had brushed past him, and he had failed to recognize it. He did not utter a word the whole way there, and he bit so hard on his pipe that he cracked the ebonite stem.

"Come in when you've parked the car."

"To the apartment?"

"No, the lodge."

There was something about the huge bulk and stony eyes of the concierge that haunted him. He found her exactly where she had been the previous day, standing at the door, holding back the net curtain. He had to push the door open before she would let go of it and step back.

She did not ask him what he wanted, but just glared at him disapprovingly.

Her skin was very white, unhealthily so. Was she just mentally deficient, a harmless "natural," such as one used to come across in country districts in the old days?

It was beginning to get on his nerves, seeing her standing there in the lodge, motionless as a pillar.

"Sit down," he said brusquely.

Unruffled, she shook her head.

"I asked you a number of questions yesterday. I am now going to repeat them, and this time I warn you that unless you tell the truth you may find yourself in serious trouble."

She did not stir, but he thought he detected a flicker of tension in her eyes. It was quite obvious that she was not afraid of him. She was afraid of no one.

"Did anyone go up to the third floor between three and four yesterday?"

"No."

"Or any of the other floors?"

"One old woman, for the dentist."

"Do you know François Paré?"

"No."

"He's a tall man, heavily built, in his fifties, balding, with a black mustache. . . ."

"I may have seen him."

"He always came on Wednesdays at about half past five. Did he come yesterday?"

"Yes."

"At what time?"

"I'm not sure. Before six."

"Was he upstairs long?"

"He came down right away."

"Did he say anything to you?"

"No."

She answered like an automaton, her face set, her stony eyes fixed unwaveringly on Maigret, as though she suspected him of wanting to trap her. Was she capable of loyalty, of lying to protect someone else? Was she aware of the significance of her testimony?

It was a matter of life and death to Florentin, for if, as she claimed, no one had entered the building, then his whole story was a tissue of lies: the ring at the doorbell, the unexpected visitor, the dash for cover in the clothes closet. There were no two ways about it: if she was telling the truth, Florentin had been the one to fire the shot.

There was a tap on the glass door. Maigret went to let Lapointe in.

"This is one of my assistants," he explained. "I repeat, think before you speak, and say nothing unless you're sure of your facts."

Never before in her life had she been called upon to play so important a part, and no doubt she was thoroughly enjoying it. For here was the Head of the Criminal Investigation Department almost pleading for her help, something which, surely, she could not have hoped for in her wildest dreams.

"You say François Paré came into the building shortly before six. Had you not seen him at all earlier in the day?"

"No."

"You're quite sure that, if he had been in, you couldn't have missed seeing him?"

"Yes."

"But there must be times when you're in your kitchen, and can't see the entrance."

"Not at that hour."

"Where is the telephone?"

"In the kitchen."

"Well, then, if it rang . . ."

"It didn't ring."

"Does the name Courcel mean anything to you?"

"Yes."

"How do you come to know Monsieur Courcel by name, and not Monsieur Paré?"

"Because he almost lived here at one time. . . . About ten years ago, he often spent the night up there, and he and the Papet woman went out a lot together."

"Did you find him friendly?"

"He would always pass the time of day."

"You seem to prefer him to the others."

"He had better manners."

"I believe he still spends the night here sometimes, usually on a Thursday?"

"That's no business of mine."

"Was he here yesterday?"

"No."

"Would you recognize his car?"

"Yes, it's blue."

Her voice was flat and toneless. Lapointe was very much struck by this.

"Do you know the name of the man with the limp?"

"No."

"Has he never been into the lodge?"

"No."

"His name is Lamotte. . . . Did you see him yesterday?"

"No."

"Nor the man with red hair, whose name is Bodard?"

"No, I didn't see him either."

Maigret would have liked to shake the truth out of her, as one shakes coins out of a money box.

"What you're saying, in other words, is that Léon Florentin was alone up there with Joséphine Papet the whole time?"

"I didn't go up to see."

It was infuriating.

"You must see that, if you're telling the truth, there's no other explanation."

"There's nothing I can do about it."

"You can't stand Florentin, can you?"

"That's my business."

"One would almost think you were determined to get even with him."

"You can think what you like."

There was something wrong somewhere. Maigret could feel it. Maybe she really was as stolid as she seemed. Possibly she could not help her monotonous voice. Perhaps she had always been a woman of few words. Even so, there was a jarring note somewhere. Either she was deliberately lying, for some reason best known to herself, or she knew more than she was telling.

Of one thing there was no doubt. She was very much on the defensive, striving to anticipate and prepare for the questions to follow.

"Tell me, Madame Blanc, has anyone been trying to intimidate you?"

"No."

"If you know Joséphine Papet's murderer, and he has threatened reprisals if you talk . . ."

She shook her head.

"Let me finish. . . . You would do well to ignore his threats. If you talk, we shall arrest him, and you will be safe from him. If not, you are running a grave risk that he may decide, at any time, that you would be better out of the way. . . ."

She looked at him with a faintly mocking expression. What did it mean?

"Few murderers will hesitate to kill a witness who knows too much for their peace of mind. . . . I could tell you of dozens of cases. . . . And there's another thing: unless you take us into your confidence, we can't protect you. . . ."

Maigret's hopes rose.

It was not so much that she was beginning to look almost human as that he thought he detected a faint tremor, an almost imperceptible softening of her expression, at any rate a hint of indecision.

He held his breath anxiously for a second or two.

"What have you to say to that?" he prompted at last.

"Nothing."

He had reached the end of his tether.

"Let's go, Lapointe."

Outside in the street, he said:

"I'm almost certain she knows something. . . . I can't help wondering if she's really as stupid as she looks."

"Where are we going next?"

He hesitated. The next step should really have been to question the insurance salesman. Failing that, he was not sure what he wanted to do. At last he said:

"The Boulevard Rochechouart."

Florentin's premises were locked up. The painter, who was at his easel in the doorway of the neighboring workshop, called across to them:

"There's no one there."

"Has he been out long?"

"He's been gone since this morning, and he didn't come back for lunch. Are you police?"

"Yes."

"I thought so. . . . Ever since yesterday, there's been someone prowling about, around here, and he's followed wherever he goes. . . . What's he done?"

"We don't know for sure that he's done anything."

"In other words, he's a suspect?"

"If you like."

He was the kind of man who wanted nothing better than to have someone to talk to. It must have been lonely for him most of the time.

"Do you know him well?"

"He stops by for a chat occasionally."

"Does he have many customers?"

The painter gave Maigret a broad grin.

"Customers? For one thing, I can't imagine where they'd come from. . . . Whoever would think of looking for an antique shop, if you can call it that, down a miserable little alley like this?

"Besides, he's hardly ever in. . . . When he does come,

it's mostly just to hang up a sign saying 'Back soon' or 'Closed until Thursday.'

"From time to time, he does spend a night in the cubbyhole, I believe.

"At least I presume he does, because sometimes I see him shaving when I arrive in the morning. . . . I live on the Rue Lamarck, myself."

"Did he ever talk about himself?"

The painter worked with rapid brush-strokes. No doubt he had painted the Sacré-Coeur so often that he could have done it blindfolded. Without pausing in his work, he considered Maigret's question.

"He couldn't stand his brother-in-law, that's for sure."

"Why not?"

"Well, according to him, if his brother-in-law hadn't cheated him, he wouldn't be where he is now. . . . His parents, it seems, had a prosperous business, I can't remember exactly where. . . ."

"In Moulins."

"You may be right. . . . When the father retired, the daughter's husband took over the business. The agreement was that he would make over a share of the profits to Florentin. However, after the father died, he never got another sou. . . ."

Maigret was thinking of the laughing, rosy-cheeked girl who used to stand behind the white marble counter. It seemed to him, in retrospect, that perhaps his visits to the shop, infrequent though they were, had been chiefly on her account.

"Did he borrow money from you?"

"How did you know? Never very large sums. . . . The fact is, I've never had much to spare. . . . Twenty francs, now and again. . . . Once or twice, but not often, as much as fifty. . . ."

"Did he pay you back?"

"He always said he would pay me back next day, but actually it was usually a day or two later. . . . What's he supposed to have done? You're Chief Superintendent Maigret, aren't you? I recognized you at once. I've often seen your picture in the papers. . . .

"If you're taking a personal interest in him, it must be something pretty serious. Murder, is it? Do you suspect him of having killed someone?"

"I just don't know."

"If you want my opinion, I don't think he's capable of murder. He's not the sort. . . . Now, if you were to say he'd been . . . well . . . careless with money . . . But even then, maybe it isn't altogether his fault. . . . He's always full of schemes, you know, and I'm sure he genuinely believes in them. . . . Some of them aren't bad, either! It's just that he gets carried away and is apt to fall flat on his face. . . ."

"You don't happen to have a key to his workshop, do you?"

"How did you know?"

"I just thought you might have."

"Of course, it's only once in a blue moon that a customer turns up, but it has been known to happen. . . . That's why he leaves a key with me. . . . He only has a few bits and pieces to sell, and I know what he wants for them."

He went indoors, opened a drawer, and returned with a massive key.

"I don't suppose he'll mind. . . ."

"You've no need to worry about that."

For the second time Maigret, assisted by Lapointe, searched the workshop and cubbyhole with meticulous care and thoroughness. A sweetish smell pervaded the narrow little room where Florentin slept, that of some brand of shaving soap unfamiliar to Maigret.

"What are we looking for, Chief?"

Crossly, Maigret replied:

"I've no idea."

"The blue Jaguar doesn't seem to have been anywhere near the Rue Notre-Dame-de-Lorette yesterday. The woman who runs the dairy nearby knows it well by sight.

" 'It's always parked just across the street on Thursdays,' she said, then as an afterthought: 'That's odd! Today is Thursday, and I haven't seen it. . . . The owner is a little fat man. . . . I hope nothing has happened to him.' "

This was Janvier, making his report.

"I also asked at the garage on the Rue La Bruyère. . . . I had a look at Joséphine Papet's car while I was at it. . . . It's a Renault, two years old. It's in very good condition and has only done fifteen thousand miles. . . . Nothing in the trunk. . . . A Michelin Guide, a pair of sun-glasses, and a bottle of aspirin tablets in the glove compartment. . . . I hope we'll have better luck with the insurance agent."

Janvier, sensing that the Chief Superintendent was still at sea over the case, pretended nonchalance and waited in tactful silence for his comments.

In the end, however, he was forced to ask: "Are you having him up here?"

"He's not expected back at his hotel until this evening. It might be a good idea if you went around there tonight, say at about eight. . . . You may have a long wait. . . . Anyway, as soon as he gets there, give me a ring at home."

It was past six. Most people had already left. Just as

Maigret was reaching for his hat, the telephone rang. It was Inspector Leroy.

"I'm in a restaurant on the Rue Lepic, Chief. He's just ordered dinner. I'll take advantage of the opportunity and have mine here too. We spent the afternoon seeing an idiotic film in a movie house on the Place Clichy. It was a continuous showing, so we made a real orgy of it, with me sitting just behind him, and saw it twice around. . . ."

"Did he seem on edge?"

"Not in the least. . . . Every now and then he turned around and winked at me. . . . If I'd given him the slightest encouragement just now, he'd have invited me to sit at his table. . . ."

"I'll send someone along to the Boulevard Rochechouart shortly, to relieve you."

"Well, you know, this isn't an exhausting assignment. . . ."

"All right, I leave it to you to get a relief. . . . I don't know who's available. And don't forget to call me as soon as the redhead gets back to his hotel. . . . It's the Beauséjour. . . . Keep out of sight as well as you can. . . ."

Maigret stopped for a drink at the bar on the Place Dauphine. A depressing day on the whole, and the worst of it had been his meeting with Victor Lamotte.

No, perhaps not the worst; he must not forget his exchange with the concierge.

"Charge it to my account."

Several of his colleagues were playing *belote* in a corner of the café. He waved to them as he went out. When he got home he made no attempt to hide his ill-humor. He could not have done so with Madame Maigret, anyway.

"When I think how much simpler it would be," he grumbled, hanging up his hat.

"What would be simpler?"

"To arrest Florentin. Anyone else, in my place, wouldn't hesitate. If the Examining Magistrate knew just half of what I know, he'd send me off to arrest him here and now."

"What's stopping you, then? Is it because you used to be friends?"

"Not friends," he corrected her. "Schoolmates."

He filled the meerschaum pipe that he never smoked except at home.

"Anyway, that's not the reason . . ."

He did not seem very sure, himself, what the true reason was.

"Everything points to him. . . . Almost too much so, if you see what I mean. . . . And I can't stand that concierge. . . ."

She repressed a strong inclination to burst out laughing. To hear him talk, one would have thought that his dislike of the concierge was a major factor in his reluctance to arrest Florentin!

"It's virtually impossible to imagine anyone nowadays leading the kind of life that girl led. . . . As for her gentlemen callers, with their regular visiting hours, it's almost beyond belief!"

He was thoroughly fed up with the lot of them, starting with Joséphine Papet, who ought to have known better than to let herself be murdered. And Florentin was no help, scattering incriminating evidence right, left, and center. Then there were Paré, with his neurotic wife, and the fat little ball-bearings tycoon, and, worst of all, the insolent cripple from Bordeaux.

But the most maddening of them all was the concierge. He could not get her out of his mind.

"She's lying. . . . I'm certain she's lying, or at least that she's got something to hide. . . . But she'll never be made to talk. . . ."

"You haven't touched your food."

There was an *omelette aux fines herbes,* succulently runny, but Maigret had not even noticed it. To follow, there was a salad flavored with garlic croutons, and finally, ripe, juicy peaches.

"You shouldn't take it so much to heart. . . ."

He gave her a preoccupied look.

"How do you mean?"

"It's almost as though you were personally involved, as though it concerned a member of your own family."

This touched a chord in him, and made him realize how absurdly he had been behaving. He felt suddenly relaxed, and was even able to muster a smile.

"You're right . . . but I can't help it, somehow. . . . I can't stand being played for a sucker. . . . And someone in this case is doing just that, and it's burning me up. . . ."

The telephone rang.

"You see!"

It was Janvier, to tell him that the insurance agent had just got back to his hotel.

Next on the agenda: the redhead. Maigret was about to put the receiver down when Janvier added:

"He's got a woman with him."

CHAPTER
FIVE

The Boulevard des Batignolles, with its double row of trees, was dark and deserted, but at the end of it could be seen the brilliant illuminations of the Place Clichy.

Janvier, the red glow of his cigarette piercing the darkness, came forward out of the shadows.

"They came on foot, arm in arm. The man is shortish, especially in the leg—a very lively character. The girl is young and pretty. . . ."

"You'd better get home to bed, or your wife will have it in for me."

A familiar smell greeted Maigret in the dim, narrow entrance, for it was in such a hotel, the Reine Morte in Montparnasse, that he had stayed when he had first come to Paris. He had wondered which dead queen the hotel had been named after. No one had been able to tell him. The proprietor and his wife had come originally from the Auvergne and had militantly enforced the ban on cooking in the bedrooms.

It was a smell of warm sheets, and of people living in close proximity to one another. A fake marble plaque beside the entrance bore the legend: *Rooms to let. Monthly, weekly, daily. All home comforts. Bathrooms.* He might have been back in the Reine Morte, where the proudly advertised bathrooms had numbered one to each floor, so that it was impossible to get near them without queuing.

Seated at a roll-top desk in the office, with the bedroom keys on a board facing her, was a woman with tow-colored hair, in dressing gown and slippers. She was balancing the accounts for the day.

"Is Monsieur Bodard in?"

Without looking up, she replied, rather grumpily:

"Fourth floor. Number sixty-eight."

There was no elevator. The stair carpet was threadbare, and the higher he climbed, the more pronounced the smell. Room 68 was at the end of the hall. Maigret knocked at the door. There was no reply at first. Then, when he had knocked for the third time, a man's voice called out irritably:

"Who's there?"

"I'd like a word with Monsieur Bodard."

"What about?"

"I should prefer to state my business in private. There's no need for the whole hotel to hear what I have to say."

"Can't you come back another time?"

"It's rather urgent."

"Who are you?"

"If you'll just open the door a bit, I'll tell you."

There was a sound of creaking bed springs. The door opened a little way, and there appeared a tousled head of curly red hair, surmounting what looked like a boxer's face. Maigret could see that the man was naked, though he was doing his best to use the door as a screen. Without a word, Maigret produced his badge.

"Do I have to go with you?" asked Bodard, showing no sign of apprehension or anxiety.

"I want to ask you a few questions."

"The fact is, I'm not alone. . . . I'm afraid you'll have to wait a few minutes. . . ."

The door slammed shut again. Maigret could hear voices and the sound of people moving about. He went down the hall and sat on the stairs to wait. It was a full five minutes before the door of number 68 was opened again.

"You can come in now."

The sheets on the brass bed were rumpled. Seated at the dressing table was a dark girl, tidying her hair. Maigret felt as though he had gone back thirty-five years, so strongly did the room recall those of the Reine Morte.

The girl was wearing nothing but a cotton dress and sandals. She seemed put out.

"You want me to go, I suppose?"

"I think you'd better," replied the man with red hair.

"How long will you be?"

Bodard looked inquiringly at Maigret.

"About an hour?"

The Chief Superintendent nodded.

"You'd better wait for me in the brasserie."

With a malevolent look, she inspected Maigret from head to foot, then grabbed her handbag and left.

"I'm sorry to have called at such an inconvenient time."

"I wasn't expecting you so soon. I thought it would take you at least two or three days to track me down."

He had not bothered to do more than slip on a pair of trousers. He was still naked from the waist up. His shoulders and chest were broad and powerful, with well-developed muscles, which made up for his lack of stature. His feet were bare, too, and Maigret noticed that he had unusually short legs.

"Please sit down."

He himself sat on the edge of the rumpled bed. Maigret took the only armchair. It was exceedingly uncomfortable.

"I presume you've seen the papers?"

"I should think everyone has, by now."

He seemed a good sort. Apparently he bore his visitor no ill-will for breaking in on his tête-à-tête. There was an easy good nature about him. He would always be ready to make the best of things, if the expression of his clear blue eyes was anything to go by. He was not the worrying kind, not the sort to take a tragic view of life.

"So you really are Chief Superintendent Maigret? I imagined you as much heavier. . . . And I certainly wouldn't have expected anyone so exalted to be going around knocking on people's doors. . . ."

"There are times when it's necessary."

"I realize, of course, that you've come about poor Josée. . . ."

He lit a cigarette.

"Have you arrested anyone yet?"

Maigret smiled at this reversal of roles. It was he who should have been asking the questions.

"Was it the concierge who put you on to me? She's not a woman, she's a monument. She reminds me of one of those marble figures on tombs. She sends a shiver down my spine. . . ."

"How long have you known Joséphine Papet?"

"Let me think. . . . We're in June, aren't we? It was the day after my birthday, so it must have been April 19th. . . ."

"How did you meet her?"

"I called at her apartment. I called at all the apartments in the building that day. It's my job, if you can call it a job. You know: 'I'm an insurance salesman and I represent So-and-So'!"

"I know. . . ."

"Each one of us has a round of three or four blocks, and we spend our whole time knocking on doors and trying to drum up business. . . ."

"Can you remember what day of the week it was?"

"A Thursday. . . . I remember because, as I said, the previous day was my birthday, and I had a horrible hang-over. . . ."

"Was this in the morning?"

"Yes, about eleven."

"Was she alone?"

"No, there was a man with her, a regular string bean, very tall and thin. He said to the woman:

" 'Well, I'd better be going.'

"He gave me a good, hard look, and then he left."

"You sell life insurance, I believe?"

"Accident policies as well. And third-party insurance. That's a fairly new gimmick, and it's not doing too badly. . . . I haven't been in the job very long. Before that, I was a waiter in a café."

"What made you change?"

"That's just it, I felt like a change. . . . I used to be a carnival barker. . . . You have to have the gift of gab for that, even more than in insurance, but insurance is more respectable. . . ."

"Were you able to interest Mademoiselle Papet?"

"Not in the sense you mean."

He chuckled.

"How then?"

"Well, to begin with, she was in her dressing gown, with her hair tied up in a scarf, and the vacuum cleaner was pulled out into the middle of the room. . . . I went into my usual patter, and all the time I was talking, I was sizing her up. . . .

"She wasn't all that young, of course, but she was a neat little armful, and I had the feeling that she didn't find me unappetizing. . . .

"She told me she wasn't interested in a life policy for the very good reason that she had no one to provide for. She had no idea what would become of her money in the end, she said.

"I suggested that she should take out an annuity to mature when she was sixty, or, better still, an accident and sickness policy."

"Did she show any interest?"

"She wouldn't commit herself, one way or the other. So, as usual, I made an all-out play for her. . . . I can't help myself. . . . It's just the way I'm made. . . . Sometimes there's a scene and I get my face slapped, but it's worth a try, even if it only comes off one time in three. . . ."

"Did you bring it off with her?"

"I should think so!"

"How long have you known the young woman who was here just now?"

"Olga? Since yesterday."

"Where did you meet her?"

"In a self-service store. . . . She's a salesgirl in the Bon Marché. . . . Don't ask me if she's any good. . . . You interrupted before I got a chance to find out. . . ."

"How often did you see Joséphine Papet, after that first time?"

"I didn't count. . . . Ten or a dozen times, perhaps."

"Did she give you a key?"

"No. I rang the bell."

"Did she fix any special day for your meetings?"

"No, she just told me that she was never there on week-ends. I asked her if the gray-haired man was her husband. She assured me he wasn't. . . ."

"Did you ever see him again?"

"Yes, twice. . . ."

"Did you ever speak to him?"

"I don't think he liked me much. . . . Each time, he just gave me a dirty look and disappeared. . . .

"I asked Josée who he was. She said:

" 'Don't bother your head about him. . . . He's rather pathetic, really. He reminds me of a stray dog. . . . That's why I took him in. . . .'

" 'All the same, you go to bed with him, don't you?' I said.

" 'What else can I do? I don't want to hurt his feelings. . . . There are times when I'm almost afraid he'll commit suicide.' "

As far as Maigret could judge, Bodard spoke with unfeigned sincerity.

"Was he the only man you ever saw in her apartment?"

"I never saw any of the others. . . . We had a pre-arranged signal. . . . If she had anyone in the apartment when I rang, she would open the door just a crack, I would say that I was selling insurance, and she would say she wasn't interested, and shut the door on me."

"Did the occasion ever arise?"

"Two or three times."

"Any particular day of the week?"

"There you have me. . . . Wait a minute, though, I've just remembered, one of the times it was a Wednesday."

"What time of day?"

"About four or half past, I think."

Wednesday was Paré's day. But the Head of Inland Waterways had told him that he never got to the Rue Notre-
Dame-de-Lorette before half past five or six.

"Did he see you?"

"I don't think so. She only opened the door a crack."

Maigret gazed at him intently. He seemed preoccupied.

"What do you know about her?"

"Let me think. . . . Occasionally, she would drop a hint
about this or that. . . . I seem to remember she told me she
was born in Dieppe."

So she had not bothered to lie to the man known as the
redhead. The Divisional Superintendent had telephoned to
Dieppe to inquire about next-of-kin in connection with the
funeral arrangements, and was informed that thirty-four years
ago, in Dieppe, a daughter, Joséphine, had been born to
Hector Papet, deep-sea fisherman, and Léontine Marchaud,
housewife. As far as was known, there was no one left of the
family in the town.

Why should she have told the truth to Bodard, when she
had lied to all the others, inventing a different tale for each
of them?

"She worked for a time in a night club, until she took up
with a man she met there, a very respectable man, an industrialist. He set her up in the apartment and lived with her
for several months. . . ."

"Did she tell you where her money came from?"

"More or less. . . . She gave me to understand that
she had several rich friends who visited her from time to
time."

"Do you know their names?"

"No. But she would say things like: 'The one with the limp

is getting to be a bit of a bore. . . . If it wasn't that I'm a little scared of him . . .' "

"Did you get the impression that she really was frightened of him?"

"She was never altogether easy in her mind. That's why she kept a revolver in her bedside table drawer."

"Did she show it to you?"

"Yes."

"So she wasn't afraid of you?"

"You're joking! Why should anyone be afraid of me?"

Why indeed? There was something very likable about him. His whole appearance was somehow reassuring, curly red hair, blue, almost violet eyes, stocky body and short legs. He looked younger than his thirty years and would probably never lose his impish charm.

"Did she give you presents?"

He got up, went over to the chest of drawers, and took out a silver cigarette case.

"She gave me this."

"What about money?"

"Well, really!"

He was affronted, almost angry.

"I don't mean to be offensive. I'm only doing my job."

"I hope you put the same question to her tame scarecrow!"

"Florentin, do you mean?"

"I didn't know his name was Florentin. . . . I mean the one who had no objection to being kept by her."

"Did she talk to you about him?"

"I'll say she did!"

"I was under the impression that she was very fond of him."

"I daresay she was, to begin with. . . . She liked having someone about the place . . . someone she could talk to, who would put up with anything, who didn't matter. Most women like to keep a pet, but usually it's a dog or a cat or a canary, if you see what I mean. . . .

"Mind you, that character, Florentin, or whatever his name is, went a bit too far. . . ."

"In what way?"

"When she first met him he gave himself out to be an antique dealer. He was down and out, but he was expecting to come into a fortune any day. . . . In those days, he really did spend some of his time buying and doing over old furniture. . . . But as time went by, he got more and more into the habit of doing nothing. . . .

"It was always the same old story: 'When I get the two hundred thousand francs owing to me . . .'

"And then he'd touch her for fifty francs or so."

"If she didn't care for him, why didn't she throw him out?"

"Well, you see, she was really very sentimental. In fact, they don't come that sentimental any more, except in romantic novels. Look! I told you how it all started, didn't I? Well, she wasn't exactly a kid any more, was she? In fact, she'd had a good deal of experience, one way and another. All the same, when it was over, she burst into tears!

"I couldn't make it out. I just sat up in bed and stared at her. Then she said, between sobs:

" 'How you must despise me!'

"I mean to say, you come across that sort of thing in old books, but it was the first time I'd ever actually heard a woman talk like that. . . .

"That Florentin fellow had her sized up all right. . . . When he felt his hold loosening, he poured it on thick, getting more sentimental than she was. . . . They used to have the most heartrending scenes. Sometimes he'd storm out, swearing that he would never come back, that she would never hear from him again, and then she'd go chasing after him to some hovel or other on the Boulevard Rochechouart, where I believe he shacks up. . . ."

There was nothing very surprising to Maigret in this character sketch of his old school friend. It was just the way Florentin had behaved when threatened with expulsion from the lycée. The story went—and it had not seemed too far-fetched at the time—that he had literally groveled at the feet of the principal, declaring between sobs that the disgrace would kill him.

"Another time he took the revolver from the bedside table drawer, and made as if he was going to shoot himself in the temple. . . .

" 'I'll never love anyone but you. . . . You're all I've got in the world.'

"D'you get the picture? For hours, sometimes for days, after one of these scenes, he'd have her just where he wanted her. . . . Then, as his self-confidence returned, so did her doubts. . . .

"But if you ask me, the real reason she didn't throw him out was that she dreaded being left alone, and there was no one to take his place. . . ."

"And then she met you."

"Yes."

"And she saw you as a possible successor?"

"I think so. . . . She used to ask me if I still had many girl friends, and sometimes she'd say: 'You do like me a little, don't you?'

"She didn't exactly throw herself at me. . . . It was more subtle than that, just a hint here and there:

" 'I suppose I must seem like an old woman to you.'

"And when I protested, she'd say:

" 'Well, I am five years older than you are, and a woman

ages more quickly than a man. . . . It won't be long before I'm a mass of wrinkles. . . .'

"Then she'd return to the subject of the antique dealer:

" 'You'd think he owned me,' she said. 'He wants me to marry him.' "

Maigret gave a start.

"She told you that, did she?"

"Yes. And she went on to say that he wanted her to invest in a bar or small restaurant somewhere near the Porte Maillot. . . . She owned a house, you know, and had quite a bit of money saved, too. . . .

"He had it in for me, apparently, and always referred to me contemptuously as Ginger or Shorty.

" 'Sooner or later,' he used to say, 'he'll be leading you by the nose.' "

"Tell me truthfully, Bodard, did you go to the Rue Notre-Dame-de-Lorette at any time yesterday afternoon?"

"I see what you're getting at, Chief Superintendent. . . . You want to know if I've got an alibi. . . . Well, I'm sorry to say I haven't. . . . For a time, I gave up seeing other girls, for Josée's sake, though I must admit it wasn't easy. . . . But yesterday morning I signed up an old gent of sixty-five for a hefty policy. . . . He was looking anxiously to the future. . . .

"The older they are, the more they worry about the future. . . .

"Well, the sun was shining, and I'd treated myself to the best lunch that money could buy, so I decided to go on the prowl. . . .

"I made for the Grands Boulevards and went into a few bars. . . . It wasn't a good beginning, but then I met up with Olga, that's the girl you saw. . . . She's waiting for me in a brasserie three doors down the street. . . . I ran into her at about seven. . . . Except for that, I haven't got an alibi. . . ."

With a laugh, he asked:

"Are you going to arrest me?"

"No. But to get back to Florentin, are you saying that, in the past few weeks, his position had become precarious?"

"I'm saying that, if I'd wanted to, I could have stepped into his shoes, but as it happened I had no wish to."

"Did he know?"

"He sensed that I was a possible rival, I'm sure of that. . . . He's no fool. . . . Besides, Josée must have dropped a hint or two. . . ."

"Surely, in the circumstances, if he'd wanted to get rid of anyone, you would have been the obvious choice?"

"You'd have thought so. . . . He couldn't have known that I'd made up my mind to say no, and that I was already gently easing my way out. . . . I can't stand sniveling women. . . ."

"Do you think he killed her?"

"I've no idea, and anyway it's no concern of mine. Besides, I know nothing about the others. . . . Any one of them might have borne her a grudge for one reason or another. . . ."

"Thank you."

"Don't mention it. . . . Tell me, I don't feel like getting dressed, would you mind awfully, on your way out, giving the chick the green light? Say I'm waiting for her up here. . . ."

Never before in his life had Maigret been asked to undertake such an errand, but the request was made with such engaging artlessness that he didn't have the heart to refuse.

"Good night."

"I hope it will be!"

He had no difficulty in finding the brasserie, which was full of regulars, playing cards. It was an old-fashioned place, and the lighting was poor. Seeing Maigret making straight for the only young girl in the room, the waiter smiled knowingly.

"I'm sorry I was so long. . . . He's waiting for you up there. . . ."

She was so taken aback that she could find nothing to say. He left her there, gaping, and had to walk all the way back to the Place Clichy before he could find a taxi.

Maigret's feeling that the Examining Magistrate, Judge Page, had only recently come to Paris proved to be correct. His office, one of those not yet modernized, was on the top floor of the Law Courts. There was an old-time atmosphere about it, reminiscent of the novels of Balzac.

His clerk was working at an unstained wooden kitchen table, to the top of which a sheet of brown paper had been fastened with thumbtacks. His own office, which could be seen through the open communicating door, was bare of furniture, though cluttered with files piled up on the floor.

Before coming up, the Chief Superintendent had taken the precaution of telephoning, to make sure that the Judge was free and willing to see him.

"Take this chair. It's the best we've got, or perhaps I should say, the least dilapidated. . . . The mate to it collapsed last week under the weight of a two-hundred-pound witness. . . ."

"Do you mind if I smoke?" Maigret asked, lighting up.

"Please do."

"All our inquiries have so far failed to locate anyone related to Joséphine Papet. She can't be kept indefinitely at the Pathologists' Laboratory. . . . It may take weeks, or even months, to discover some second or third cousin. Don't you think, in the circumstances, Judge, that the best thing would be to make arrangements for the funeral without further delay?"

"Since she was not without means . . ."

"That reminds me, I deposited the forty-eight thousand francs with the Clerk of the Court, because I wasn't too happy about keeping it locked up in my office.

"With your permission, I'll get in touch with a firm of undertakers right away."

"Was she a Catholic?"

"According to Léon Florentin, who lived with her, she wasn't. At any rate, she never went to Mass."

"Have the account sent to me. . . . I'm not quite sure what the procedure is. . . . Make a note of it, Dubois."

"Yes, Your Honor."

The moment Maigret had been dreading had come. He had not attempted to stave it off. On the contrary, he himself had asked to see the Judge.

"You must have been wondering why I haven't let you have an interim report. The truth is that, even now, I'm far from sure I'm on the right track."

"Do you suspect the man who lived with her? What's his name again?"

"Florentin. All the evidence points to him, and yet I still have the gravest doubts. . . . It all seems too easy, somehow. . . . Besides which, by an odd coincidence, he and I were at school together in Moulins. . . . He's by no means a fool; in fact, I should say that he had all his wits about him, rather more than most. . . .

"Admittedly, he's a failure, but that's because of a flaw in his personality. . . . He resents all authority and is totally incapable of self-discipline. . . . As I see it, he lives in a fantasy world, a kind of imaginary puppet theater, in which nothing and no one is to be taken seriously. . . .

"He has a police record. . . . Rubber checks . . . Fraud . . . He did a year's stretch in prison. . . . But, in spite of it all, I still don't believe him capable of committing murder. . . . Or at any rate, he's incapable of bungling it. . . . If he'd done it, he would have taken very good care to cover his tracks. . . .

"All the same, I'm keeping a round-the-clock watch on him."

"Does he know?"

"He takes it as a compliment, and makes a point of turning around in the street every so often, to wink at the man on his tail. . . . He always was the clown of the class. . . . You must know the type."

"There's one in every school."

"The trouble is that, in a man of fifty, that sort of behavior isn't a joke any longer. . . . I've tracked down Joséphine Papet's other lovers. . . . One is a highly placed civil servant with a neurotic wife. . . . The other two also are men of standing and considerable wealth. . . . One lives in Bordeaux, the other in Rouen. . . .

"Needless to say, each of these men imagined himself to be the only one privileged to visit the apartment on the Rue Notre-Dame-de-Lorette. . . ."

"Have you undeceived them?"

"I've done more than that. I arranged, this morning, for each of them to receive a personal summons to a meeting in my office at three o'clock this afternoon.

"I have also summoned the concierge to attend, because I'm quite sure in my own mind that she's hiding something. I hope, by tomorrow, to have definite news for you."

A quarter of an hour later Maigret was back in his office, instructing Lucas to make arrangements for the funeral. Then, taking a bank note out of his wallet, he murmured:

"Here, see that there are some flowers on the coffin."

The sun had been shining brilliantly for days, and today was no exception, but a high wind had suddenly blown up, causing the trees outside to shake violently, and making it impossible to have the window open.

No doubt all those who had been summoned to the forthcoming meeting were shaking in their shoes. Little did they know that Maigret was even more uneasy than they were. True, it had been something of a relief to unburden himself to the Examining Magistrate, but he was still very much a prey to conflicting emotions.

There were two people constantly in the forefront of his mind. One, needless to say, was Florentin, who, it almost seemed, had piled up evidence against himself out of sheer mischief. The other was that old witch of a concierge, who haunted him like a nightmare. As far as she was concerned, he was taking no chances. Knowing that she was quite capable of ignoring his summons, he was sending an inspector to fetch her.

Realizing that it would be best to put the case out of his mind for the time being, he settled down grudgingly to his neglected paperwork and soon became so immersed in it that when he next looked up to see the time, he was surprised to find that it was ten to one.

He decided not to go home for lunch, and telephoned his wife to tell her so. Then he strolled across to the Brasserie Dauphine and sat down in his usual corner. Several of his colleagues were there having a drink at the bar, as well as a number of people he knew from other departments.

The proprietor himself came over to take his order.

"There's *blanquette de veau*. How will that do?"

"Fine."

"And a carafe of our special rosé?"

He lingered over his meal, soothed by the low murmur of voices, which was punctuated by an occasional burst of laughter. As usual, the proprietor brought him a small glass of Calvados, "on the house," with his coffee, and he made it last until it was time to go back to his office.

At a quarter to three he went into the inspectors' duty room to fetch some chairs, which he set out in a semicircle facing his desk.

"I don't want any slip-up, Janvier. You're to go and fetch her, and then take her into a room by herself, and keep her there until I send for you."

"I'm not sure I'll be able to fit her into the car all in one piece," Janvier jested.

The first to arrive was Jean-Luc Bodard. He was in high good humor. At the sight of the row of chairs, however, he frowned.

"What's this, a family reunion or a council of war?"

"A bit of both."

"You don't mean you're bringing together all . . ."

"Precisely."

"Well, it suits me all right but how do you think the others will take it? You'll get a few dirty looks, I shouldn't wonder."

And indeed the next comer, ushered in by old Joseph, after he had looked around the room turned to Maigret with a look of unpleasant surprise.

"I came in response to your summons, but I wasn't told . . ."

"You're not the only person concerned, I'm afraid, Monsieur Paré. Take a seat, won't you?"

As on the previous day, he was dressed all in black. He

held himself stiffly and was more tense than he had been in his own office. He kept darting anxious glances at the young man with red hair.

There followed an awkward pause lasting two or three minutes, during which no one spoke a word. François Paré had taken the chair nearest the window and sat with his black hat balanced on his knees. Jean-Luc Bodard, wearing a loud checked sports jacket, was watching the door as though the others couldn't come soon enough, as far as he was concerned.

The next to arrive was Victor Lamotte, very much on his dignity. Furiously he turned on Maigret:

"What's this? A trap?"

"Please be seated."

Maigret, ignoring the undercurrents, was playing the gracious host, faintly smiling, imperturbable.

"You've no right to . . ."

"You will have every opportunity of complaining to my superiors in due course, Monsieur Lamotte. Meanwhile, I'd be obliged if you would take a seat."

Florentin was brought in by an inspector. The setup was no less of a surprise to him than to the others, but his reaction was a loud guffaw.

"Well, I must say . . ."

He looked Maigret straight in the eye and gave him an appreciative wink. He thought he knew every trick in the book, but this beat them all!

"Gentlemen," he said, bowing with mock solemnity to the assembled company.

He sat down next to Lamotte, who at once shifted his chair as far away from him as possible.

The Chief Superintendent looked at the time. The three o'clock chimes sounded, and a few more minutes went by before Fernand Courcel appeared in the doorway. What he saw was such a shock to him that he spun around, as though to take flight.

"Come in, Monsieur Courcel. Sit down. . . . We're all here now, I think. . . ."

Young Lapointe was seated at one end of the desk, ready to take down in shorthand anything of interest that might be said.

Maigret sat down, lit his pipe, and murmured:

"Do smoke, if you wish."

The only one to do so was the red-haired young man. Maigret looked with interest from one to another. They were an ill-assorted lot. In a sense, they fell naturally into two groups. In the first group were Florentin and Bodard, whom Josée had truly loved, and who were now engaged in sizing each other up. They represented, in effect, age and youth, the old and the new.

Did Florentin know that the young man with red hair could have ousted him, had he so wished? If so, he did not appear to bear him any grudge. If anything, he seemed rather to approve of him.

In the second group were the three men who had visited the Rue Notre-Dame-de-Lorette in pursuit of an illusion. Their plight was much the more serious.

This was the first time that they had ever met, and yet not one of them deigned so much as to glance at the others.

"Gentlemen, you can be in no doubt as to why you are assembled here. You have all been good enough to answer my questions separately, and I, in my turn, have given you the true facts of the situation, as far as I know them.

"There are five of you present, every one of whom has, for a longer or shorter period, known Joséphine Papet intimately."

He paused for an instant. No one stirred.

"Apart from Florentin and, to a limited extent, Bodard, none of you knew of the existence of the others. That is so, is it not?"

The only response was from Bodard, who nodded. As for Florentin, he looked as though he was enjoying himself hugely.

"The fact is that Joséphine Papet is dead, and that one of you killed her."

Monsieur Lamotte half rose from his seat and began:

"I protest . . ."

To judge from his expression, he was near to storming out of the room.

"Kindly keep your protests until later. Sit down. So far, I have accused no one. I merely stated a fact. All but one of you deny having set foot in the apartment between three and four on Wednesday afternoon. . . . Not one of you, however, can establish an alibi. . . ."

Paré raised his hand.

"No, Monsieur Paré, yours won't do. I sent one of my men to have another look at your office. There is a second door, leading onto a corridor. You could have gone out that way without anyone seeing you. What's more, if any of your staff had gone into your office and found it empty, they would naturally have assumed that you had been called away by the Permanent Under-Secretary. . . ."

Maigret relit his pipe, which had gone out.

"Obviously, I can hardly expect one of you to stand up and confess his guilt. I am simply telling you what is in my mind. I am convinced not only that the murderer is here in this room, but also that there is present someone who knows who he is, and who, for some reason that escapes me, is keeping that knowledge to himself."

He looked from one to another of them. Florentin's eyes were turned toward the group in the middle, but it was impossible to tell whether his attention was fixed on anyone in particular.

Victor Lamotte was staring intently down at his shoes. He was very pale, and his face seemed all hollows and shadows.

Courcel, poor man, was trying to smile, but all he could manage was a pathetic little grimace.

Bodard was looking thoughtful. It was clear that he had been much struck by Maigret's last remark, and was trying to sort things out in his own mind.

"Whoever killed Josée must have been well known to her, since she received him in her bedroom. But Josée was not alone in the apartment. . . ."

This time they all looked at one another and then, with one accord, turned to stare uneasily at Florentin.

"You're quite right. . . . Léon Florentin was there when the doorbell rang, and, as he had been forced to do on other occasions, he took refuge in the clothes closet. . . ."

Maigret's old school friend was making a violent effort to maintain his air of unconcern.

"Did you hear a man's voice, Florentin?"

He addressed him as *"vous,"* but on this occasion, at least, Florentin could scarcely object.

"I couldn't hear much in there, just a murmur of voices. . . ."

"What exactly happened?"

"I'd been there about a quarter of an hour when I heard a shot."

"Did you rush into the bedroom to see what was the matter?"

"No."

"Did the murderer leave at once?"

"No."

"How long was he in the apartment after the shot?"

"About a quarter of an hour."

"Did he take the forty-eight thousand francs from the drawer of the desk?"

"No."

Maigret saw no necessity to disclose that it was Florentin himself who had made off with the money.

"The murderer must have been looking for something. Every one of you, I presume, must have had occasion to write to Josée, if only to cancel an appointment, or to keep in touch while you were away on holiday."

Once more he looked from one to another. They shifted uneasily, crossing or uncrossing their legs.

He was now concentrating his attention on the three solemn-faced men who had most to lose in terms of family, position, and reputation.

"What about you, Monsieur Lamotte, did you ever have occasion to write to her?"

"Yes," he muttered under his breath. He was barely audible.

"The social world in which you move in Bordeaux has changed very little with the times, I should imagine. If my information is correct, your wife is a very rich woman in her own right and, according to the scale of values accepted in Les Chartrons, comes from a family even more distinguished than your own. Have you ever been threatened with exposure by anyone?"

"I simply cannot permit . . ."

"And you, Monsieur Paré, did you ever write to her?"

"Yes, as you suggested, when I was on holiday. . . ."

"You are, I believe, in spite of your visits to the Rue Notre-Dame-de-Lorette, very much attached to your wife. . . ."

"She's a sick woman. . . ."

"I know. . . . And I'm sure you would go to great lengths to spare her the anguish . . ."

Paré clenched his teeth. He seemed on the verge of tears.

"And now, Monsieur Courcel, what about you?"

"I may have scribbled a note to her once or twice. . . ."

"Which, I'm sure, would leave no one in any doubt as to the nature of your relations with Joséphine Papet. . . . Your wife is younger than you are, and of a jealous disposition, I assume. . . ."

"What about me, then?" broke in the redhead, making a jest of it.

"You could have had an altogether different reason for wanting to get rid of her."

"Not jealousy, at any rate," he protested, and turned to the others as if for moral support.

"Josée could have told you about her savings. You may have known that she didn't deposit her money in a bank but kept it in the apartment."

"If so, then surely I would have taken it?"

"Not if you were interrupted while you were still searching for it."

"Do I look as if I'd do a thing like that?"

"Most of the murderers I've met have looked very much like anyone else. . . . As to the letters, you could have taken them with the intention of blackmailing the signatories. . . .

"Because the letters have vanished, all of them, possibly including some from people we haven't even heard of. You'd expect most women, by the age of thirty-five, to have accumulated quite a volume of correspondence. . . . But there was nothing in Joséphine Papet's desk except bills. Every single one of your letters, gentlemen, has been spirited away, and by one of you. . . ."

They were all so anxious to appear innocent that none of them succeeded in looking anything but thoroughly guilty.

"I am not inviting the murderer to stand up and confess. I shall simply remain here in the confident hope that, within the next few hours, the man who knows who murdered Josée will come to see me. . . .

"Even so, that may not be necessary. . . . There is still one witness missing, and that witness also knows who the murderer is. . . ."

Maigret turned to Lapointe.

"Get Janvier, will you?"

There was a long pause, during which not a sound was heard. The five men held their breath, scarcely daring to move. Suddenly, the room felt very hot. When at last Madame Blanc made her entrance, resembling more than ever a piece of monumental sculpture, the effect was electric.

She was wearing a dress of spinach green, with a red hat perched on the very top of her head, and the handbag she was carrying was almost as big as a suitcase. She stood for a moment, framed in the doorway, her face stony, her expressionless eyes darting from one to another of those present.

When she had taken them all in, she turned her back on them, and it was all Janvier could do to prevent her from leaving. For a moment, it looked as if they might come to blows.

In the end the woman gave way and came into the room.

"I still have nothing to say," she announced, glowering malevolently at Maigret.

"I think you know all these gentlemen?"

"I'm not being paid to do your job for you. Let me go."

"Which of these men did you see going toward the elevator or the stairs, between three and four in the afternoon on Wednesday?"

Then a strange thing happened. This stubborn, stony-faced woman was unable to prevent her lips from twitching in a faint ghost of a smile. All of a sudden she was looking distinctly smug, there was no doubt about it. It was almost as though she had won a victory.

They were all looking at her. Maigret was watching them, hoping to detect signs of special anxiety in one of their faces. But he could not tell which of them was most affected. Victor Lamotte was pale with suppressed fury. Fernand Courcel, in contrast, was very flushed; Maigret had noticed his rising color for some minutes past. As for François Paré, he was simply overwhelmed with shame and misery.

At last Maigret spoke.

"Do you refuse to answer?"

"I have nothing to say."

"Make a note of that, Lapointe."

She shrugged and, still with that enigmatic glint of triumph in her eyes, said contemptuously:

"You can't frighten me."

CHAPTER
SIX

Maigret stood up, looked at each of them in turn, and concluded:

"Gentlemen, I'm grateful to you all for coming here. It is my belief that your time has not been wasted, and I have no doubt that I shall be hearing from one of you shortly."

He cleared his throat.

"In conclusion, for those who are interested, I am now in a position to inform you that the funeral of Joséphine Papet will take place tomorrow morning. The hearse will set out from the Pathologists' Laboratory at ten o'clock."

Victor Lamotte, still fuming, was the first to go. He did not even glance at the others and, needless to say, took no leave of the Chief Superintendent. No doubt his chauffeur-driven limousine was waiting for him below.

Courcel hesitated a moment, then, with a nod, went out. François Paré, as though he scarcely knew what he was saying, murmured:

"Thank you . . ."

The redhead was the only one to offer his hand. He bounded up to Maigret, exclaiming appreciatively:

"You certainly don't pull your punches!"

Florentin alone hung back. Maigret said to him:

"You wait here a minute. . . . I shan't be long."

He left Lapointe, who had not moved from his seat at the end of the desk, to keep an eye on him, and went into the inspectors' room next door. Torrence was there, a bulky figure seated at his typewriter, transcribing a report. He typed with two fingers and applied himself to the task with intense concentration.

"I want the house on the Rue Notre-Dame-de-Lorette watched. . . . See to it at once, will you? I want the name of everyone who goes in or comes out. . . . If any one of the men who have just left my office turns up, he's to be followed inside."

"Is something worrying you?"

"I'm quite sure the concierge knows more than is good for her. I don't want her to come to any harm."

"What about Florentin? Do we go on keeping a check on him?"

"Yes. I'll let you know when I've done with him."

He went back to his office.

"You can go, Lapointe."

Florentin was standing at the window, hands in his pockets, looking very much at home. He was wearing his usual expression of ironic detachment.

"Say, if you didn't rattle them! I've never enjoyed myself so much in all my life!"

"Is that so?"

For it had not escaped Maigret that there was something very forced about this display of high spirits.

"The one who really took my breath away was the concierge. . . . Talk about getting blood out of a turnip! Do you really think she knows?"

"I hope so, for your sake."

"What do you mean?"

"She maintains that no one went upstairs between three and four. . . . Unless she changes her mind, I shall have no choice but to arrest you, because if what she says is true, you're the only person who could have done it."

"What was the point of the confrontation?"

"I was hoping one of them would panic."

"Aren't you concerned that I might be in danger, too?"

"Did you see the murderer?"

"I've already told you I didn't."

"Did you recognize his voice?"

"No. I've told you that too."

"Then what have you got to worry about?"

"I was in the apartment. Thanks to you, they all know that now. The murderer can't be sure I didn't see him."

Casually, Maigret opened a drawer in his desk and took out the pack of photographs that Moers had sent down to him from Criminal Records. He glanced through them, and handed one to Florentin.

"Take a look at that."

The baker's son from Moulins, assuming an air of bewilderment, examined the photograph carefully. It was of a corner of the bedroom, showing the bed, and the bedside table with its drawer half open.

"What am I supposed to be looking for?"

"Doesn't anything strike you?"

"No."

"Remember your first statement. The doorbell rang. . . . You bolted into the clothes closet. . . ."

"It's the truth."

"Very well, let's assume, for the sake of argument, that it is. According to you, Josée and her visitor barely paused in the living room and went straight on through the dining room into the bedroom. . . ."

"That's right."

"Let me finish. Also according to you, they were together in the bedroom for nearly a quarter of an hour before you heard the shot."

Florentin, frowning, examined the photograph again.

"That photograph was taken very soon after the murder. . . . Nothing in the room had been touched. . . . Look at the bed. . . ."

A little color rose in Florentin's wasted cheeks.

"Not only has the bed not been turned down, but there isn't so much as a dent or a crease on the counterpane."

"What are you getting at?"

"I'll tell you. Either the visitor merely wanted to talk to Josée, in which case they would have stayed in the living room, or he came for some other purpose. And since the condition of the bed suggests that it wasn't the usual purpose, perhaps you can tell me what, in actual fact, they were doing in the bedroom?"

"I don't know. . . ."

Maigret could almost see his mind working, as he thought up plausible answers.

"Just now, you mentioned letters. . . ."

"Well?"

"Maybe he came to ask for his letters back. . . ."

"Are you suggesting that Josée would have refused to give them to him? Do you think it likely that she would have tried to blackmail a man who was making her a generous monthly allowance?"

"They could have gone into the bedroom for the usual reason, and then quarreled. . . ."

"Listen to me, Florentin. I know your statements by heart. . . . I felt from the very beginning that there was something wrong somewhere. . . . Did you take those letters as well as the forty-eight thousand francs?"

"I swear I didn't. . . . If I had, surely you'd have found them, just as you found the money. If I'd had the letters, I'd have hidden them in the same place."

"Not necessarily. . . . It's true that you were frisked to make sure you hadn't got the revolver, but you weren't searched. I know you're an excellent swimmer, don't forget, and I also know that you took a sudden dive into the Seine. . . ."

"I was fed up with everything. . . . I realized that you suspected me. . . . And besides, I'd just lost the only person in the world who . . ."

"I'd be obliged if you'd spare me the crocodile tears."

"When I jumped off that parapet, my only thought was to end it all. It was just a foolish impulse. One of your fellows was on my tail."

"Precisely."

"What do you mean by that?"

"Suppose that, when you hid the money on top of the wardrobe, you'd momentarily forgotten about the letters, which were still in your pocket? You couldn't take the risk of their being found in your possession. How could you have explained them away?"

"I don't know."

"You realized that a constant watch would be kept on you from then on. But if you were to jump into the Seine, ostensibly in a fit of despair, you could easily get rid of the incriminating papers. . . . They only needed to be weighted with a pebble or something of the sort, to sink safely to the bottom."

"I never had the letters."

"I agree, that's one possibility. If true, it would certainly explain what the murderer was doing in the apartment during the quarter of an hour after the shot. But there's another thing that's worrying me. . . ."

"What am I being accused of now?"

"The fingerprints . . ."

"I daresay mine were all over the apartment, but what do you expect?"

"That's just it, there were no fingerprints in the bedroom, neither yours nor anyone else's. Now we know you opened the desk to get at the money. And presumably the murderer opened at least one drawer when he was looking for the letters. . . . At any rate, he can't have spent a quarter of an hour in the room without touching anything. . . .

"Which can only mean that, after he'd gone, all the smooth surfaces, including the door handles, were wiped—by you."

"I don't understand. . . . I did no such thing. . . . Who's to say that someone didn't sneak in and do it after I'd left? There was plenty of time, while I was on my way to the Boulevard Rochechouart, or coming to see you at the Quai des Orfèvres."

Maigret did not reply. Noticing that the wind had dropped, he went over and opened the window. There followed a long silence, then Maigret said very quietly:

"When did your notice expire?"

"What notice? What on earth are you talking about?"

"Your notice to quit the apartment . . . to part from Josée . . . in other words, to get out. . . ."

"There was never any question . . ."

"Oh, yes, there was, and well you know it. . . . You were beginning to show your age and, what's more, you were becoming greedy. . . ."

"I suppose that swine of a redhead told you that?"

"What does it matter?"

"It couldn't be anyone else. He's been worming himself into her good graces for weeks."

"He has a job. He works for his living."

"So do I."

"Your so-called antique business is only a front. How many pieces of furniture do you sell in a year? Most of the time there's a 'Closed' sign on your door."

"I have to be out and about, buying."

"No. . . . Joséphine Papet had had about as much as she could take. For want of anything better, she was planning to install Bodard in your place."

"It's his word against mine."

"I know you from way back, Florentin. Your word isn't worth *that*. . . ."

"You *have* got it in for me, haven't you?"

"Why should I 'have it in for you,' as you put it?"

"You always did, even in Moulins. . . . My parents owned a prosperous business. . . . I always had money to spend. . . . But what was your father? Just a sort of upper servant on the Château de Saint-Fiacre estate. . . ."

Maigret flushed and clenched his fists. He could have hit him, for if there was one thing he could not tolerate it was a slur on his father's name. Maigret Senior had, in actual fact, been steward of the estate, with responsibility for twenty or more farms.

"You're despicable, Florentin."

"You asked for it."

"The only reason I'm not having you locked up right now is that I haven't yet got the tangible evidence I need, but it won't be long now. . . ."

He strode across to the door of the inspectors' room and flung it open.

"Which of you is in charge of this scoundrel here?"

Lourtie stood up.

"Keep close behind him, and when he gets home keep a watch at the door. You can arrange for relief among yourselves."

Florentin, realizing that he had gone too far, looked very much abashed.

"I apologize, Maigret. . . . I lost my head and didn't know what I was saying. . . . Put yourself in my shoes. . . ."

The Chief Superintendent maintained a grim silence and kept his eyes averted as Florentin went out. Almost immediately after he had gone, the telephone rang. It was the Examining Magistrate wanting to know the outcome of the confrontation.

"It's too early to say," explained Maigret. "It's rather like dragging a pond. I've stirred up a lot of mud, but I can't tell yet what may come up. . . . I've arranged the funeral for ten tomorrow morning."

A number of newspapermen were hanging about in the corridor. He was unusually short with them.

"Are you on the track of the killer, Superintendent?"

"There's more than one track."

"And you're not sure which is the right one?"

"That's right."

"Do you think it's a *crime passsionel*?"

It was on the tip of his tongue to say that there was no such thing, because that was more or less what he believed. In his experience, a lover scorned or a woman slighted was more often driven to murder by hurt pride than by thwarted passion.

That evening he and Madame Maigret sat watching television and sipping their little glasses of *framboise,* from the bottle sent to them by his sister-in-law in Alsace.

"What do you think of the movie?"

He almost said:

"What movie?"

Certainly he had been watching the screen. There had been a lot of movement and bustle and agitation, but if he had been asked to summarize the plot he could not have done it.

Next morning, with Janvier at the wheel of the car, he arrived at the entrance of the Pathologists' Laboratory just before ten.

Florentin, looking taller and thinner than ever, was standing at the edge of the sidewalk with a cigarette dangling from his lips. Beside him was Bonfils, the inspector who had relieved Lourtie.

Florentin gave no sign of having seen the police car draw up. He just stood there with hunched shoulders, utterly dejected, as though he would never again be able to look the world in the face.

The hearse was at the door, and the undertaker's men wheeled the coffin over to it on a handcart.

Maigret opened the rear door of the car.

"Get in!"

And, turning to Bonfils:

"You can go back to the Quai. . . . I'll look after him."

"Are we ready?" inquired the undertaker's man.

They set off. In the rear mirror, the Chief Superintendent caught sight of a yellow car, which seemed to be following them. It was a cheap, much-battered, little open two-seater. Above the windshield Jean-Luc Bodard's mop of red hair was clearly visible.

They drove in silence toward Ivry, and almost the entire length of the great, sprawling cemetery. The grave was in one of the new extensions, where trees had not yet had time to grow. Lucas had not forgotten to order flowers, as Maigret had asked him, and the red-haired young man had also brought a wreath.

As the coffin was being lowered from the hearse, Florentin buried his face in his hands, his shoulders shaking. Was he really weeping? Not that it meant anything. He had always been able to shed tears to order.

It was to Maigret that the undertaker's man handed the spade, for him to shovel the first sods of earth into the grave. A few minutes later the two cars were starting up for the trip back.

"The Quai des Orfèvres, Chief?"

Maigret nodded. Florentin, in the back of the car, still did not say a word.

When they reached the forecourt of the Quai des Orfèvres, Maigret got out of the car and said to Janvier:

"You'd better stay with him until Bonfils comes down to take over."

From the back of the car came an anguished cry:

"I swear to you, Maigret, I didn't kill her!"

Maigret merely shrugged and walked away slowly, through the glass doors, toward the staircase. He found Bonfils in the inspectors' duty room.

"I've left your customer downstairs. . . . He's all yours."

"What shall I do if he insists on walking side by side with me?"

"That's up to you, only don't lose sight of him."

To his surprise, when he went into his office he found Lapointe waiting for him. He looked worried.

"I've got bad news, Chief."

"Not another murder?"

"No. The concierge has vanished."

"I gave orders that she should be kept under close watch!"

"Lourtie called up half an hour ago. He was almost in tears. . . ."

He was one of the oldest inspectors on the Force, and he knew every trick of the trade.

"How did it happen?"

"Lourtie was standing on the sidewalk opposite the building when she came out. She didn't have a hat on, and she was carrying a marketing bag.

"She didn't even look around to see if she was being followed. First, she went into the butcher's and bought a cutlet. . . . They seemed to know her there. . . .

"Still without looking around, she went on down the Rue Saint-Georges, stopping to go into an Italian grocer's. While she was in there, Lourtie stayed outside, walking up and down.

"When, after a quarter of an hour or more, she hadn't reappeared, he began to get worried and went into the shop. It's very long and narrow, and there's another entrance at the back, opening onto the Square d'Orléans and the Rue Taitbout. Needless to say, the bird had flown.

"After he'd spoken to me, Lourtie went back to resume his watch on the building. As he said, there was no point in trying to search the whole district. . . . Do you think she's flown the coop?"

"I'm quite sure she hasn't."

Maigret was back at the window, looking out onto the

chestnut trees, and listening to the birds twittering in the branches.

"She didn't murder Joséphine Papet, so why on earth should she try to escape? Especially since she took nothing with her except her marketing bag, not even a hat!

"She must have been going to meet someone. . . . I rather suspected she might, after the confrontation yesterday. . . .

"I was convinced from the start that she'd seen the murderer, either when he arrived or when he left, or both. . . .

"Suppose that, as he was leaving, he saw her there with her nose pressed against the glass, and those extraordinary eyes of hers staring at him. . . ."

"I see what you mean!"

"He knew that she was bound to be questioned. And he, remember, was a regular visitor to Joséphine Papet's apartment, and therefore known to the concierge."

"Do you think he used threats?"

"Threats would cut no ice with a woman of that sort. You saw what she was like yesterday afternoon. . . . On the other hand, I can't see her being able to resist a bribe. . . ."

"If she's already had money out of him, why the disappearing trick?"

"Because of the confrontation."

"I don't understand."

"The murderer was here in this room. . . . She saw him. . . . She had only to say the word for him to be arrested. . . . But she preferred to say nothing. . . . It's my belief that she suddenly woke up to the fact that her silence was worth a great deal more than she had been paid. . . .

"So she decided, this morning, to raise her price, but she couldn't do much about it with a police inspector at her heels. . . .

"Get me the hall porter at the Hôtel Scribe."

As soon as he was put through, Maigret grabbed the receiver.

"Hello! Hôtel Scribe? Is that the hall porter? Chief Superintendent Maigret speaking. . . . How are you, Jean? . . . The children all well? . . . Good. . . . Splendid. . . . I'm interested in one of your regulars, name of Lamotte, Victor Lamotte, yes. I presume his suite is booked by the month? . . . Yes, that's what I thought. . . .

"Put me through to him, will you. . . . What's that? . . . Did you say yesterday? . . . The express to Bordeaux? . . . I thought he always stayed until Saturday night. . . .

"Has anyone been asking for him this morning? You haven't by any chance had an inquiry from a very fat woman, shabbily dressed, carrying a marketing bag?

"No, I'm serious. . . . You're quite sure? . . . Oh, well, thanks all the same, Jean."

He knew the hall porters of all the big hotels in Paris, some ever since they had joined the staff as bell-hops.

The Blanc woman had not gone to the Hôtel Scribe, and even if she had done so she would not have found the wine-grower there.

"Get me his office on the Rue Auber."

He was determined to leave nothing to chance. The offices on the Rue Auber were closed on Saturdays, but there was one member of the staff in the building, catching up on a backlog of work. He had not set eyes on the boss since two o'clock the previous afternoon.

"Try the offices of Courcel Frères, Ball Bearings, on the Boulevard Voltaire."

No reply. Here, on Saturdays, there was not even a caretaker on duty.

"Try his home in Rouen. . . . Don't utter the word 'police.' I just want to know if he's in."

Fernand Courcel occupied the whole of an old house on the Quai de la Bourse, a stone's throw from the Pont Boïeldieu.

"May I speak to Monsieur Courcel, please?"

"He's just gone out. This is Madame Courcel speaking. . . ."

She had a pleasant, youthful voice.

"May I take a message?"

"Do you know when he'll be back?"

"He'll be in for lunch. . . . We've got people coming. . . ."

"I take it he only got back this morning?"

"No, last night. . . . Who is speaking?"

In view of Maigret's injunction, Lapointe judged it wiser to ring off.

"He's just gone out. . . . He got back last night. . . . He's expected home for lunch. . . . They've got people coming. . . . His wife sounds charming."

"That only leaves François Paré. . . . Try his number in Versailles."

Here, too, a woman's voice answered. She sounded tired and fretful.

"Madame Paré speaking."

"Could I speak to your husband?"

"Who is calling?"

"A member of his staff," said Lapointe, telling the first lie that came into his head.

"Is it important?"

"Why do you ask?"

"Because my husband is in bed. . . . When he got back

last night, he wasn't feeling well. . . . He had a very restless night, so I thought it best to keep him in bed today. . . . He works too hard for a man of his age. . . ."

The inspector, sensing that she was about to hang up on him, hastily came to the point:

"Has anyone been asking for him this morning?"

"What do you mean?"

"Has anyone called to see him on business?"

"No one at all."

Without another word, she hung up.

Florentin and the redhead had been at the cemetery at the time of Madame Blanc's disappearance, and she had not been in touch with any of the other three suspects.

Madame Maigret, sensing that he had enough on his mind already, decided that he was not to be worried further until he had had his lunch. It was not until she had poured his coffee that she asked:

"Have you seen the paper?"

"I haven't had time."

There was a morning paper on a table in the living room. She went to get it and handed it to him.

He read the banner head:

THE MURDER
ON THE RUE NOTRE-DAME-DE-LORETTE

And below, two somewhat more informative subtitles:

Mysterious gathering at the Quai des Orfèvres

Chief Superintendent Maigret baffled

He gave a groan and went off to get his pipe before settling down to read the story.

Yesterday's edition of this paper carried the full story of the murder committed in an apartment on the Rue Notre-Dame-de-Lorette.

The victim was a young, unmarried woman, Joséphine Papet, occupation unknown.

We ventured to suggest that the killer was probably one of several men who had enjoyed the favors of the murdered girl.

In spite of the stubborn silence of the Criminal Investigation Department, we are given to understand that a number of persons were summoned to the Quai des Orfèvres yesterday, to attend a meeting which was in the nature of a confrontation. Among those present, we are told, were several men of standing and influence.

Our attention has been drawn to the fact that one of the suspects, in particular, was in the apartment at the time of the murder, and the question arises: Is he the guilty man, or merely a witness to the crime?

It is a source of some embarrassment to Chief Superintendent Maigret, who is personally in charge of the case, that the man in question, Léon F. . . . ., is an old school friend.

Can this be the reason why, in spite of the evidence against him, the man is still at large? It seems hard to credit. . . .

Maigret, grinding his teeth, crushed the paper up into a ball.

"Idiots!" he muttered.

Was it possible that one of his own inspectors had in all innocence committed an indiscretion, led on by the wily gentlemen of the press? He was all too familiar with the methods of newspapermen. They would certainly have left no stone unturned. There was no question but that they must have interviewed the concierge, and it was not unlikely that she had been a good deal more forthcoming with them than with the police.

There was also the bearded painter, Florentin's next-door neighbor on the Boulevard Rochechouart.

"Does it matter so much?"

He shrugged. Anyway, the only effect of the article was to make him more than ever reluctant to act precipitately.

Before leaving the Quai, he had received the ballistics report from Gastinne-Renette. This confirmed the opinion of the pathologist. The bullet was enormous, of twelve-millimeter caliber. There were very few in existence, and it could only have been fired from an obsolete revolver of Belgian make, which would not be obtainable from an ordinary gunsmith.

The writer of the report had commented that it would be impossible to fire such a weapon with any degree of accuracy.

There was no doubt that the murder weapon was the old gun from Josée's bedside table. Where was it now? It would be a waste of time to search for it. It could be anywhere, in the river, in some drain or other, on a rubbish dump, or in a field in the country.

What could have possessed the murderer to remove so compromising an object, instead of leaving it where it was? Possibly, in his haste to get away, he had not had time to remove all trace of fingerprints.

If that were so, then he would not have had time, either, to wipe his fingerprints from the surfaces he had touched in the apartment.

Yet the fact remained that all the surfaces in the bedroom, including the door handles, had been wiped clean.

Was it, therefore, to be concluded that Florentin was lying when he claimed that the murderer had stayed in the apartment for a quarter of an hour after the shot had been fired?

Was it not more likely that Florentin himself had wiped away the prints?

Whatever Maigret's line of reasoning, it always led back to Florentin. He was the obvious suspect. But the Chief Superintendent distrusted the obvious.

All the same, he was ashamed of himself for allowing Florentin so much latitude. It almost smacked of favoritism, he felt. Had he not, perhaps, been unconsciously influenced by a sort of loyalty to his own youth?

"It's perfectly ridiculous!" he exclaimed aloud.

"Were you really such friends?"

"Not at all. . . . I used to find all that clowning rather irritating."

He did not mention the fact that he used sometimes to go into the shop just to catch a glimpse of Florentin's sister. It almost made him blush, even now.

"See you later."

She put up her face to be kissed.

"Will you be back for dinner?"

"I hope so."

He had not noticed that it had started to rain. His wife caught up with him on the stairs and gave him his umbrella.

He boarded a bus on the corner of the Boulevard and stood on the platform, swaying with the motion of the vehicle and gazing absently at the people hurrying to and fro along the sidewalks. What queer cattle human beings were, ready to break into a run at the slightest provocation! Where did they think they were going? What was all the rush for?

"If I'm no further ahead by Monday, I'll put him under lock and key," he promised himself, as a sop to his conscience.

He put up his umbrella and walked from the Châtelet to

the Quai des Orfèvres. The wind was blowing in squally gusts, driving the rain full into his face. This was what he used to refer to as "wet water" when he was a child.

No sooner was he in his office than there was a knock at the door, and Lourtie came in.

"Bonfils has taken over from me," he said. "She's back."

"What time did she get in?"

"Twenty past twelve. . . . I saw her coming down the street, as cool as you please, carrying her marketing bag. . . ."

"Was it full?"

"A good deal fuller and heavier than it was this morning. . . . She didn't even deign to look at me as she went past. I think she was trying to needle me. She made straight for the lodge and took down the sign saying: 'Concierge at work on staircase.' "

Maigret paced back and forth between the window and the door at least half a dozen times. Then, abruptly, he halted. He had come to a decision.

"Is Lapointe there?"

"Yes."

"Tell him to wait for me. I won't be a minute."

He took a key from his drawer, the one that opened the communicating door between his department and the Law Courts. He made his way down several long corridors and up a dark staircase to the Examining Magistrate's office. He knocked at the door.

Most of the offices in this part of the building were empty and silent. He was not very hopeful of finding Judge Page still at work on a Saturday afternoon.

"Come in," said a voice, sounding a long way off.

Maigret found the Judge, covered with dust, in the little

windowless room adjoining his office, struggling to get things in some sort of order.

"Would you believe it, Maigret, there are documents here, two years old or more, that have never been filed? It will take me months to clear up the mountain of papers left behind by my predecessor."

"I've come to ask you to sign a search warrant."

"Just give me time to wash my hands."

The nearest washbasin was at the far end of the corridor. Maigret warmed to him. A thoroughly decent, conscientious fellow.

"Any new developments?"

"I've had trouble with the concierge. That woman knows a great deal, I'm sure of it. . . . Yesterday, when I had them all together, she was the only one who didn't turn a hair. What's more, I believe she's the only one, apart from the murderer himself, who knows who did it."

"Why won't she talk? Is it just because she looks upon the police as her natural enemies?"

"I don't think that would be enough to keep her quiet, considering the risk. . . . It wouldn't have surprised me if the killer had tried to get rid of her. . . . In fact, with that possibility in mind, I've put a watch on the building. . . .

"It's my belief that she's been paid to keep her mouth firmly shut, though I don't know how much. . . .

"As soon as the crucial importance of her evidence was brought home to her, she must have realized that she hadn't been paid enough. . . .

"So this morning she gave my inspector the slip with all the cunning of a professional. . . . She set the scene first by going into the butcher's, so that my man naturally assumed that she was just doing her ordinary shopping, and then she went into the grocer's. . . . He, of course, suspected nothing, and waited outside for her, for a quarter of an hour, only to discover that the shop had two entrances, and that she'd slipped out by the back way."

"Do you know where she went?"

"Florentin was with me at the cemetery at Ivry, and so was Jean-Luc Bodard. . . ."

"Did she call on any of the others?"

"Well, she certainly didn't see any of them. Lamotte went back to Bordeaux yesterday on the evening express. . . . Courcel is in Rouen, and was giving a luncheon party. As for Paré, he's in bed ill, and his wife is worrying about him, for a change. . . ."

"Whose name do you want on the search warrant?"

"Madame Blanc, the concierge. . . ."

The Judge went over to his clerk's table and took a warrant from the drawer. He filled it in, signed and stamped it.

"Good luck."

"Thanks."

"Incidentally, don't worry about all that stuff in the papers. . . . No one who knows you . . ."

"Thank you."

A few minutes later he was driving away from the Quai des Orfèvres, with Lapointe at the wheel. The traffic was heavy, and everyone seemed even more in a hurry than usual. It was always the same on a Saturday. In spite of the rain and the wind, they couldn't wait to get out of town, onto the highways, into the country.

For once, Lapointe had no trouble in parking. There was a convenient space just across the road from the house. The lingerie shop was shut. The shoeshop was still open, but there was no one in it. The proprietor was standing in the doorway, gloomily watching the rain pouring down.

"What are we looking for, Chief?"

"Anything we can make use of, but chiefly money."

For the first time, Maigret found Madame Blanc sitting down inside the lodge. She was wearing a pair of steel-rimmed glasses on the end of her bulbous nose and reading the early edition of the afternoon paper.

Maigret went in, followed by Lapointe.

"Did you wipe your feet?"

And as they did not reply, she muttered:

"What do you want this time?"

Maigret handed her the search warrant. She read it through carefully, twice.

"I don't know what it means. What are you going to do?"

"Search."

"You mean you're going to go through all my things?"

"I apologize."

"I'm not sure I oughtn't to get a lawyer."

"If you do, it will only suggest that you have something to hide. . . . Keep an eye on her, Lapointe, and see that she doesn't touch anything."

Against one wall of the lodge was a Henri II-style dresser. The top half was a cupboard with glass doors, in which were displayed some tumblers, a water jug, and a pottery coffee set decorated in a bold flower pattern.

In the right-hand drawer there were knives, forks, and spoons, a corkscrew, and three napkin rings of various shapes and sizes. The tableware had once been silver-plated, but it was now so worn that it looked more like brass.

The left-hand drawer proved more interesting. It was stuffed with papers and photographs. One of the photographs was of a young couple, presumably Monsieur and Madame Blanc, though she was scarcely recognizable. It must have been taken when she was about twenty-five. Although, even at that age, she was plump, no one could have foreseen that she would grow into the mountain of flesh that she was today. As for Monsieur Blanc, at whom she was actually smiling in the picture, his chief distinguishing feature was a fair mustache.

Neatly folded in an envelope was a list of the tenants, with the rents they paid, and, under a stack of postcards, a post-office savings book.

It went back many years. At the beginning, the sums deposited were small, ten or twenty francs at a time. Later, she had got into the habit of saving fifty francs a month regularly, except for January, when the annual tips from the tenants raised the sum to between a hundred and a hundred and fifty francs.

The total amounted to eight thousand, three hundred and twenty-two francs, and a few centimes.

There were no very recent entries. The last was a fortnight old.

"Much good may that do you!"

Ignoring her, he went on with his search. In the lower half of the dresser, there was a dinner service, and, beside it, a pile of folded checked tablecloths.

He lifted the velvet cloth draped over the round table, to see if there was a drawer underneath, but he found none.

To his left there was a television set on a table. He opened the drawer of the table but found nothing except a few bits of string and some nails and thumbtacks.

He went into the room in back, which served a double purpose as kitchen and bedroom. The bed stood in an alcove, concealed by a shabby curtain.

He began with the bedside table and found, in the drawer, a rosary, a prayer book, and a sprig of rosemary. For a moment he could not imagine what the rosemary was doing there, then he remembered the custom of sprinkling the dead with holy water and could only suppose that she had kept it in memory of one of her parents.

It was hard to think of that woman as ever having been a wife to anyone, but undoubtedly she had once been somebody's child, like everyone else.

He had known others like her, men and women, whom life had so hardened that they had almost been turned into monsters. For years now, she had been confined, by day and by night, to these two dark, airless rooms, with scarcely more freedom of movement than she would have had in a prison cell.

As for any communication with the outside world, she saw no one except the postman, and the tenants going in and out.

Every morning, regardless of her weight and swollen legs, she had to clean out the elevator and sweep the stairs from top to bottom.

If, tomorrow or the next day, she would no longer be able to work, what then?

And here he was, harassing her. He felt ashamed of himself. He opened the door of the little refrigerator. Inside was half a cutlet, the remains of an omelette, two slices of ham, and a few vegetables, no doubt those she had bought that morning.

On the kitchen table stood a half-bottle of wine. It only remained now for him to search the cupboard. Here he found nothing but underclothes and dresses, a corset, and a pair of elastic stockings.

It was painful to him now to have to continue the search, but he was unwilling to admit defeat. She was not the woman to be fobbed off with promises. If anyone had bribed her to keep her mouth shut, he must have paid her there and then, in cash.

He went back into the lodge, and when she saw him her eyes flickered, revealing a twinge of anxiety that she was unable to hide.

It was enough to tell him that there was nothing for him to find in the kitchen. Very slowly, he surveyed the lodge. Where was it that he had failed to look?

He made a sudden dive for the television set, on top of which were stacked a few periodicals. One of these was devoted to radio and television programs, with accompanying articles and illustrations.

The moment he picked it up he knew that he had won.

It fell open of its own accord at the place where she had slipped in three five-hundred franc and seven hundred-franc notes.

Two thousand, two hundred francs. The five-hundred franc notes were brand-new.

"I'm entitled to my savings, am I not?"

"I've seen your savings book, don't forget."

"What of it? Who says I have to put all my eggs in one basket? I might find myself needing ready money at any time."

"Two thousand, two hundred francs isn't exactly petty cash!"

"That's my business. Just try making trouble for me, and see where it gets you. . . ."

"You're a good deal cleverer than you make yourself out to be, Madame Blanc. . . . I have a shrewd suspicion that you were expecting me today, search warrant and all. . . . If you had deposited the money, the transaction would have been entered in your savings book, and I could not have failed to be struck by the unusually large sum, and the date. . . .

"You could have put the money in a drawer or a cupboard, or have sewn it into your mattress, but no. Have you

by any chance read the works of Edgar Allan Poe? You chose
to slip the notes between the pages of a magazine. . . ."

"I'm not a thief."

"I'm not suggesting that you are. In fact, I don't believe
you asked for this money. It's my opinion that the murderer,
seeing you at the door of the lodge as he was going out, came
in and offered it to you, before you even knew that a murder
had been committed in the building. . . .

"There was no need for him to volunteer any explanation.
. . . He only had to ask you to forget you had seen him on
that occasion. . . .

"You must have known who he was, otherwise he would
have had nothing to fear from you. . . ."

"I have nothing to say."

"Yesterday, when you saw him in my office, you realized
that he was a very frightened man, and that the person he
was afraid of was none other than yourself, you being the
only one in a position to give him away.

"It didn't take you long to figure it out that a man,
especially if he is rich, probably values his liberty at a good
deal more than two thousand, two hundred francs. So you
decided to find him this morning and see how much more you
could get."

As on the previous day, her lips twitched in a faint ghost
of a smile.

"You found no one there. . . . You had forgotten that
today is Saturday."

The expression of the woman's bloated face, at once stubborn and enigmatic, did not change.

"I'm not saying anything. Beat me up if you like. . . ."

"I'd rather not, thank you. We'll meet again. Let's go,
Lapointe."

The two men went out and got into the little black car.

CHAPTER
SEVEN

Sunday was a gloomy day, with a glimmer of pale sunlight filtering through massed banks of cloud. In spite of this, they followed the crowds streaming out into the country for the day.

When they had first bought the car, it had been their intention to use it only for going to and from their little house in Meung-sur-Loire and for touring on vacations. They had, in fact, been to Meung three or four times, but it was really too far to go there and back in a day. There was no one to look after the house in their absence, which meant that Madame Maigret just had time to do a little dusting and prepare a quick meal, before it was time to leave.

It was about ten in the morning when they set out.

They had agreed that it would be best to keep off the highways.

Unfortunately, thousands of other Parisians had come to the same conclusion, and the little country roads that ought to have been so delightful were as crowded as the Champs-Elysées.

They were looking for an attractive little inn, with an appetizing menu. They knew from long experience that most of the wayside inns were always full to overflowing and that those which were not served frightful food, but this did not deter them from trying again, Sunday after Sunday.

It was the same as with the television set. When they had first bought it, they had vowed that they would only look at programs that really interested them. At the end of a fortnight, Madame Maigret had taken to setting the table in such a way that they were both able to face the screen during dinner.

They did not bicker in the car, as so many married couples do. All the same, Madame Maigret was very tense at the wheel. She had only recently passed her driving test and was still lacking in self-confidence.

"Why don't you pass them?"

"There's a double white line."

On this particular Sunday, Maigret scarcely said a word. He sat slumped in his seat, puffing at his pipe, his eyes fixed on the road ahead, glowering. In spirit, he was on the Rue Notre-Dame-de-Lorette, reconstructing the events leading up to the death of Joséphine Papet in as many different ways as he could think of

He considered each hypothetical reconstruction in turn, having built it up with great attention to detail, even to the extent of inventing appropriate dialogue. Then he tested its validity from every angle. Each time, just when it was beginning to seem impregnable, some flaw would appear, and he was back where he started.

It was like trying to solve a chess problem, with the people involved as the pieces, which could be moved here or there to produce this or that result.

Time and again he set up the problem, rearranging the

pieces in different positions, sometimes removing one or several of them, sometimes bringing new ones into play.

They stopped for lunch at an inn. The food was no better and no worse than what was to be had at any railway station buffet. The only difference was the size of the bill.

They set out for a walk in the woods, but they were discouraged by mud underfoot and a steady downpour of rain.

They got home early, to a dinner of cold cuts and vegetable salad. Maigret was so restless that his wife suggested that they go to the movies, which they did.

At nine o'clock sharp on Monday morning he was in his office. The rain had stopped, and the sun, though not very bright, was shining.

The reports of the inspectors who had taken turns keeping watch on Florentin were on his desk.

Florentin had spent Saturday evening in a brasserie on the Boulevard de Clichy. This, it seemed, was not one of his usual haunts, because no one there seemed to recognize him.

He had ordered a beer and taken it over to a table next to a party of four regulars, who were obviously old friends, and who were immersed in a game of *belote*. He had sat for some time with his elbow on the table and his chin in his hand, following the game in an absent-minded way.

At about ten, one of the card-players, a weedy little man who had been chattering away ceaselessly the whole evening, suddenly said:

"I'm sorry, fellows, but I must be going. . . . My woman will skin me alive if I'm home late, especially since I'm going fishing tomorrow."

The others pressed him to stay, but to no avail. When he had gone, they had looked about them for someone to make a fourth.

One of them had asked Florentin, in a strong southern accent:

"Do you play?"

"I'll join you with pleasure."

Thereupon he had moved over to the vacant seat at the table and stayed there, playing *belote* until midnight, while poor Dieudonné, whose shift it was, sat gloomily slumped in a corner.

And Florentin, always the gentleman, had stood drinks all around, thus making a substantial dent in the hundred francs that Maigret had given him.

He had gone straight home from the brasserie and, with a final conspiratorial wink at Dieudonné, had gone to bed.

He had slept late, and had not gone into the tobacconist's for his breakfast of croissants dipped in coffee until after ten. Dieudonné, by that time, had been relieved by Lagrume, and Florentin had looked him up and down with interest, as much as to say: "This is a new one on me!"

Lagrume was the gloomiest of all the inspectors, and not without reason: he never seemed to be without a cold for more than a couple of months in the year, besides which he was afflicted with flat feet, which gave him endless trouble, and caused him to walk in a most peculiar way.

From the tobacconist's Florentin had gone into a betting shop, where he had invested in a lottery ticket, after which he had sauntered off down the Boulevard des Batignolles. He had gone past the Hôtel Beauséjour without so much as a glance. There was no reason to suppose that he knew that the redhead lived there.

He had lunched in a restaurant on the Place des Ternes, then, as on the previous Friday, he had gone to a movie.

What was to become of this tall, thin man with the mobile

india-rubber face, when the Chief Superintendent's hundred francs were exhausted?

He had not met a single person he knew. No one at all had tried to get in touch with him. He had gone into a cafeteria for his dinner, and then straight home to bed.

As to the Rue Notre-Dame-de-Lorette, there was nothing of any interest to report from there either. Madame Blanc had emerged from the lodge only to sweep the stairs and put out the garbage cans.

Some of the tenants had gone to Mass, others had gone out for the day. All in all, it had been a boring and frustrating day for the two inspectors on watch outside in the street, which on a Sunday had been virtually deserted.

Maigret was devoting this Monday morning to rereading all the reports on the case, in particular those of the pathologist, the ballistics expert, Moers, and Criminal Records.

Janvier, after a discreet knock on the door, came in, looking fresh, cheerful, and ready for anything.

"How do you feel, Chief?"

"Rotten."

"Didn't you enjoy your Sunday?"

"No."

Janvier could not help smiling. He was well acquainted with this mood, and as a rule it was a good sign. It was Maigret's way, when he was working on a case, to soak everything up like a sponge, absorbing into himself people and things, even of the most trivial sort, as well as impressions of which he was perhaps barely conscious.

It was generally when he was close to saturation point that he was at his most disgruntled.

"How did you spend the day?"

"We went to my sister-in-law's, my wife and I and the kids.

. . . There was a fair in the market place, and the children spent a small fortune shooting at clay pigeons. . . ."

Maigret got up and started pacing the room. A buzzer sounded summoning Heads of Departments to the weekly conference for the exchange of information.

"They can perfectly well get along without me," grumbled Maigret.

He was in no mood to answer the questions that his Chief would undoubtedly ask, nor to give him advance warning of his plans, which were anyway somewhat nebulous. He was still feeling his way.

"If only that frightful woman could be made to talk!"

The huge, phlegmatic concierge was still in the forefront of his mind.

"There are times when I regret the abolition of third-degree methods. I'd like to see just how long she'd hold out."

He didn't seriously mean it, of course. It was just his way of letting off steam.

"What about you? Have you any ideas?"

Janvier never liked it when Maigret asked him point-blank for his opinion. Somewhat hesitantly, he ventured:

"I think . . ."

"Come on, out with it! You think I'm barking up the wrong tree, is that it?"

"Not at all. It's just that I have a notion that Florentin knows even more than she does. . . . And Florentin is in a much weaker position. He's got nothing to look forward to. . . . If he's able to pick up a few sous here and there by loafing around Montmartre, he'll be lucky. . . ."

Maigret looked at him with interest.

"Go and get him."

As he was leaving, Maigret called him back.

"And you'd better pick up the concierge from the Rue Notre-Dame-de-Lorette at the same time, while you're about it. She'll raise Cain, but never mind, use force if necessary. . . ."

Janvier smiled. He could not quite see himself coming to blows with that great mountain of a woman, who was at least twice his weight.

Soon after he left, Maigret was on a telephone line to the Ministry of Public Works.

"I'd be obliged if you would put me through to Monsieur Paré."

"Hold on, please."

"Hello! Is that Monsieur Paré?"

"Monsieur Paré isn't in today. . . . His wife has just called up. . . . He's not at all well."

Maigret hung up and dialed the Versailles number.

"Madame Paré?"

"Who's speaking?"

"Chief Superintendent Maigret. How is your husband?"

"Not at all well. . . . The doctor has just left. . . . He's afraid he may be on the verge of a nervous breakdown."

"It wouldn't be possible for me to talk to him, would it?"

"The doctor recommends complete rest."

"Does he seem worried? Has he asked to see the newspapers?"

"No. He's just withdrawn into himself. . . . I can scarcely get a word out of him. . . ."

"Thank you."

Next he telephoned the Hôtel Scribe.

"Is that you, Jean? Maigret here. . . . Is Monsieur Victor Lamotte back from Bordeaux yet? . . . So he's left for his office already, has he? . . . Thanks."

He dialed the number of Lamotte's office on the Rue Auber.

"Chief Superintendent Maigret speaking. Would you put me through to Monsieur Lamotte, please."

There was a great deal of clicking on the line. Apparently it was necessary to go through a whole hierarchy of subordinates to get to the great man himself.

Finally, a voice said dryly:

"Yes?"

"Maigret here."

"So I was told."

"Will you be in your office all morning?"

"I really can't say."

"I'd be obliged if you'd stay there until you hear from me again."

"I'd better warn you that, if I'm summoned to your office again, I shall have my lawyer with me this time."

"You'll be perfectly within your rights."

Next, Maigret tried the Boulevard Voltaire, but Courcel had not yet arrived.

"He never gets in before eleven, and sometimes he doesn't come in at all on a Monday. Would you care to speak to the assistant manager?"

"No, that's all right."

Pacing up and down the room with his hands behind his back, and glaring from time to time at the clock, Maigret once again reviewed all the possibilities that he had considered in the car on the previous day.

He eliminated each in turn, until only one was left. This, subject to the tying up of a few loose ends, provided the answer.

Looking more than a little shamefaced, he opened the cupboard in which he always kept a bottle of brandy. It was not intended for his own use, but as a restorative, to be produced in case of need, as when, for instance, someone he was questioning collapsed after making a confession.

He could not claim to be in a state of collapse. It was not he who was going to have to make a confession. Nevertheless, he took a long swig straight from the bottle.

Having done so, he felt thoroughly ashamed of himself. Once more, he glanced impatiently at the clock. Then, at long last, he heard footsteps in the corridor, and a voice raised in furious anger, which he recognized as that of Madame Blanc.

He crossed to the door and opened it.

Florentin, though visibly uneasy, attempted, as usual, to laugh it off:

"This place is beginning to feel like a home away from home for me!"

As for the woman:

"I'm a free citizen, and I demand . . ." she thundered.

"Take her away and lock her up somewhere, Janvier. You'd better stay with her, but take care she doesn't scratch your eyes out."

And, turning to Florentin:

"Take a seat."

"I'd rather stand."

"And I'd rather you sat down."

"Oh, well, if you insist . . ."

He made a face, just as he used to in the old days, after an altercation with one of the teachers, trying to restore his self-esteem by raising a laugh.

Maigret went into the other room to get Lapointe. He had been present at most of the earlier interviews and was familiar with all the details of the case.

Taking his time over it, the Chief Superintendent filled his pipe, lit it, and gingerly pressed down the smoldering tobacco with his thumb.

"I take it, Florentin, that you have nothing to add to your statement?"

"I've told you all I know."

"No."

"It's the truth, I swear it."

"And I know it's a pack of lies, from start to finish."

"Are you calling me a liar?"

"You always were a liar. Even at school . . ."

"It was only for a laugh . . ."

"Agreed. . . . But this is no laughing matter."

He looked his old school friend straight in the eye, with a very grave expression, in which there was something of contempt and also something of pity. But probably more of pity than contempt.

"What will become of you?"

Florentin shrugged.

"How should I know?"

"You're fifty-three."

"Fifty-four. . . . I'm a year older than you are. I had to repeat the sixth grade."

"You're getting a bit shopworn. . . . It won't be easy to find another Josée."

"I shan't even try."

"Your antique business is a flop. . . . You have no skills, no training, no professional experience. . . . And you're too seedy to play the confidence game any longer. . . ."

It was cruel but it had to be said.

"You're a miserable wreck, Florentin."

"Everything always went sour on me. . . . I know I'm a failure, but . . ."

"But you won't admit defeat, will you? You're still hoping
. . . what for, for heaven's sake?"

"I don't know. . . ."

"Right. That's settled, then. And now the time has come
for me to take a weight off your mind."

There was a long pause, during which Maigret looked
searchingly into the face of his old school friend. Then he
came out with it:

"I know you didn't kill Josée."

CHAPTER
EIGHT

It came as much less of a surprise to Florentin than to Lapointe. He shot up in his seat, aghast, with his pencil poised in mid-air, and gaped at his Chief.

"But that doesn't mean you've got anything to crow about. Your conduct has been far from blameless. . . ."

"But you yourself admit . . ."

"I admit that, on that one point, you've told the truth, which, I must confess, is more than I'd have expected of you. . . ."

"I can explain . . ."

"I'd rather you didn't keep interrupting. Last Wednesday, probably around a quarter past three, as you say, someone rang the doorbell of the apartment. . . ."

"You see!"

"Do please shut up. . . . As usual, not knowing who it might be, you made a bolt for the bedroom. . . . Since you and Josée were not expecting any callers, you listened. . . .

"I take it that one or another of her lovers did occasionally change the time of his visit?"

"In that case, they would always telephone. . . ."

"Didn't they ever turn up unexpectedly?"

"Very rarely."

"And on those rare occasions, you hid in the clothes closet. On Wednesday, however, you were not in the clothes closet but in the bedroom. . . . You recognized the voice of the caller, and you took fright. . . . Why? Because you realized that it wasn't Josée he had come to see, but you."

Florentin froze. It was clear that he could not make out what process of reasoning had led his old school friend to this conclusion.

"I have proof, you see, that he went up to the apartment on Wednesday. . . . Because the gentleman in question, having just committed a murder, panicked and tried to buy the concierge's silence with the sum of two thousand, two hundred francs, which was all he had on him at the time. . . ."

"But you yourself have admitted that I'm innocent!"

"Of the murder. . . . But that isn't to say that you weren't indirectly the cause of it. . . . If one can speak in terms of morality where you're concerned, one could say that you were morally responsible."

"I don't understand."

"Yes you do."

Maigret stood up. He never could sit still for long. Florentin followed him with his eyes, as he paced up and down the room.

"Joséphine Papet had fallen in love with someone new. . . ."

"You surely don't mean the redhead?"

"I do."

"It was just a passing fancy. . . . He'd never have agreed to her terms, living with her, skulking in closets, keeping out of the way when necessary. . . . He's young. . . . He can have all the girls he wants. . . ."

"That doesn't alter the fact that Josée was in love with him, or that she'd had enough of you. . . ."

"How do you know? You're only guessing."

"She said so herself."

"Who to? Not to you. You never saw her alive."

"To Jean-Luc Bodard."

"And you really believe every word that fellow says?"

"He had no cause to lie to me."

"What about me, then?"

"You faced the risk of a longish prison sentence . . . probably as much as two years, in view of your previous convictions."

Florentin took this more calmly. Although he had not realized just how much Maigret had discovered about his past, he had heard enough to be prepared for the worst.

"To get back to the Wednesday caller . . . The reason you were so badly shaken when you recognized his voice was that, some days or weeks earlier, you had attempted to blackmail one of Josée's lovers.

"Needless to say, you picked on the one who seemed to you the most vulnerable, in other words the one who set the greatest store by his reputation. You raised the subject of his letters. . . .

"How much did you get out of him?"

Florentin hung his head, looking very sorry for himself.

"Nothing."

"You mean he wouldn't play?"

"No, but he asked for a few days' grace."

"How much were you asking for?"

"Fifty thousand. . . . I needed at least that. . . . I wanted to make a clean break, to get away and start life over somewhere else. . . ."

"So I was right. Josée was trying to ease you out as gently as possible."

"Maybe she was. . . . She certainly wasn't the same, any more. . . ."

"Now you're beginning to talk sense. Keep it up, and I'll do my best to see that you're let off as lightly as possible in the circumstances."

"Would you really do that for me?"

"What a fool you are!" muttered Maigret in an undertone, not intending Florentin to hear. But he did hear, and flushed crimson to the roots of his hair.

It was no more than the truth. There were literally thousands of people like him living in Paris, subsisting on the borderline of crime by more or less openly exploiting the naïveté or cupidity of their fellow men.

Such people were always full of grandiose schemes, the realization of which was thwarted only by the lack of a few thousand or a few hundred thousand francs.

Most of them managed, in the end, to cheat some poor chump out of his money, and then there would follow a brief spell of prosperity, of fast cars and expensive restaurants.

When the money was spent, they were back where they started, and the whole laborious process would begin again. And yet scarcely one in ten of such people ever saw the inside of a corrective institution or a prison.

Florentin was the exception. All his schemes had come to nothing, and the last had proved the most disastrous of all.

"Now, will you tell the rest of the story, or would you rather I did?"

"I'd rather leave it to you."

"The visitor asks to see you. He knows you are in the apartment, because he's made it his business to find out from the concierge. He is unarmed. He's not especially jealous, and he has no wish to kill anyone. . . .

"All the same, he is in a highly excitable frame of mind. Josée, nervous on your account, denies that you are in the apartment and claims to have no idea where you are.

"He goes into the dining room, heading for the bedroom. You retreat into the bathroom with the intention of hiding in the closet."

"But I never got that far."

"Right. . . . He marches you back into the bedroom."

"Shouting at the top of his voice that I was despicable, beneath contempt," interposed Florentin, bitterly. "And with her there, listening."

"She knows nothing about the blackmail business. She doesn't understand what's going on. You tell her to keep out of it. . . . But, in spite of everything—because you feel it's your last chance—you still cling to the hope of getting that fifty thousand francs. . . ."

"I'm not sure of anything any more. . . . It was all so confused. . . . I don't think any of us quite knew what was happening. There was Josée, pleading with us to calm down. . . . The man was in a furious temper. I'd refused to give him back his letters. When he saw that I meant it, he pulled open the bedside table drawer and grabbed the revolver. . . .

"Josée began screaming. I admit, I was scared, too, and . . ."

"And you got behind her?"

"I swear to you, Maigret, it was sheer accident that she was hit. . . .

"You could see the fellow didn't know the first thing about

handling guns. . . . He kept waving it about. . . . I was actually on the point of giving him back his damned letters when it went off. . . .

"He looked utterly stunned. . . . He made a queer little gurgling noise in his throat, and bolted out of the room."

"Did he still have the revolver?"

"I presume so. . . . At any rate, when I looked for it, it was gone. . . . As soon as I bent down to look at Josée, I knew she was dead. . . ."

"Why didn't you call the police?"

"I don't know. . . ."

"I do. . . . You were thinking about the forty-eight thousand francs she kept in a biscuit box, the tin box you wrapped in newspaper and took back to your workshop. . . . Incidentally, it was very careless of you to use that day's morning paper. . . .

"As you were leaving, you remembered the letters and stuffed them in your pocket. . . .

"At last, you had riches within your grasp. . . . For the man whom you had blackmailed by threatening to expose an affair with a woman had now committed a murder. . . ."

"What on earth put that idea into your head?"

"The fact that you removed the fingerprints on the furniture and door handles. It wouldn't have mattered if your prints had been found—even you never attempted to deny that you were in the apartment. No, it was the other man's prints that you were anxious to get rid of, because once he was identified and caught, he could be of no further use to you."

Maigret returned to his chair, sat down heavily, and refilled his pipe.

"You went back to your place and hid the biscuit box on top of the wardrobe. . . . For the time being, you forgot about the letters in your pocket. Then, suddenly, you thought of me, your old school friend, who would surely protect you, at least from rough handling. . . . You always were something of a physical coward. Remember? . . . There was that kid Bambois. . . . As I recall, he only had to threaten to twist your arm to have you shaking in your shoes. . . ."

"Now, you're being cruel."

"Look who's talking! If you hadn't been such a louse, Josée would be alive today."

"I'll never forgive myself, as long as I live."

"That won't bring her back. . . . Anyway, it's entirely between you and your conscience. You came here with every intention of misleading me, but you'd scarcely opened your mouth before I realized there was something wrong somewhere.

"I had the same feeling in the apartment. . . . The whole setup was phony. It was as though I'd been handed a tangled ball of string but couldn't find the end that would help me straighten it out.

"Of all the people concerned in this case, the concierge intrigued me most. She's a great deal tougher than you are."

"She never could stand the sight of me."

"Any more than you could stand the sight of her. By keeping her mouth shut about the caller, not only did she stand to gain two thousand, two hundred francs, but she had you just where she wanted you. As to your dive into the Seine, that was sheer folly. If it hadn't been for that, I might never have thought of the letters. . . .

"It was clear from the start that you had no intention of drowning. No one who could swim as you can would attempt suicide by throwing himself off the Pont-Neuf when it was crawling with people, knowing, moreover, that he would hit the water within a few feet of a boat moored to the bank.

"You suddenly remembered those letters in your pocket.

. . . One of my men was close on your heels. . . . At any moment, you might be searched. . . ."

"I never dreamed you'd guess . . ."

"It's my job, and I've been at it thirty-five years," muttered Maigret.

"The secret is never to let oneself be taken in," he added, and went out to have a word with Lucas.

When he returned to his office, he found a Florentin with all the stuffing knocked out of him. He was just a long, lean husk of a man, with hollow cheeks and sunken eyes.

"Am I right in thinking that I'll be charged with attempted blackmail?"

"That depends . . ."

"On what?"

"On the Examining Magistrate. . . . And, to some extent, on me. . . . Don't forget that, by obliterating the fingerprints, you were obstructing the police and laying yourself open to a further charge of being an accessory after the fact. . . ."

"You wouldn't do that to me, surely?"

"I'll have a word with the Judge. . . ."

"I could probably survive a year or, at the most, two in prison, but if it were a question of being shut up for years, then I'd have to be carried out feet first. . . . I have heart trouble, as it is. . . ."

No doubt he would do his utmost to be allowed to serve his sentence in the infirmary of La Santé Prison. And this man had once been the boy Maigret had known in Moulins, who had kept them all in gales of laughter. He could always be relied on to brighten up a dull hour, with the whole class egging him on.

And they always had egged him on, knowing how much he delighted in thinking up new practical jokes and displaying himself in an infinite number of different guises.

The clown . . . There had been that time when he had pretended to drown in the Nièvre. They had spent a quarter of an hour searching for him, and found him, at last, hiding in a clump of reeds to which he had swum under water.

"What are we waiting for?" he asked, suddenly anxious again.

It was certainly a relief to him to have got it over, but he was by no means confident that his old friend might not, even now, have a change of heart.

There was a knock at the door, and old Joseph came in and handed a visiting card to Maigret.

"Show him up. And go and ask Janvier to bring in the woman."

He would have given anything for a tall, cool glass of beer, or even another nip of brandy.

"Allow me to introduce my lawyer, Maître Bourdon."

One of the leading lights of the legal profession, a former President of the French Bar, whose name had been put forward for membership in the Academy.

With icy dignity, Victor Lamotte, dragging his foot a little, crossed the room and sat down. He scarcely glanced at Florentin.

"I presume, Superintendent, that you have good and sufficient reasons for insisting on the presence of my client here today? I understand that on last Saturday, also, he was summoned to attend a meeting here, and I should warn you that, on my advice, he reserves his position as to the legality of those proceedings. . . ."

"Won't you sit down, Maître?" said Maigret tersely.

Janvier propelled Madame Blanc into the room. She seemed much agitated. Then she caught sight of the lame man, and froze.

"Come in, Madame Blanc. Please sit down."

She had been taken completely unaware, or so it seemed.

"Who is that?" she asked, pointing to Maître Bourdon.

"Your friend Monsieur Lamotte's lawyer."

"Have you arrested him?"

Her protuberant eyes seemed more prominent than ever.

"Not yet, but I intend to do so in a moment. Do you identify him as the man who, last Wednesday, came down from Mademoiselle Papet's apartment and paid you two thousand, two hundred francs to keep your mouth shut?"

She was silent, her lips pressed together in a straight, hard line.

"You were very ill advised to give her that money, Monsieur Lamotte. So large a sum was bound to put ideas into her head. It didn't escape her that if her silence was worth so much to you before she had even asked for anything, its real value was probably higher. . . ."

"I have no idea of what you're talking about."

The lawyer was frowning.

"Let me explain how I arrived at the conclusion that it was you, rather than any of the other suspects, who were guilty of the murder. . . .

"I have kept Madame Blanc under observation for several days. On Saturday, she managed to shake off the inspector who was following her, by going into a shop and slipping out through the back entrance. . . . Her intention was to see you and demand more money. . . . The matter, you see, was pressing, as she had no means of knowing how long it would be before you were arrested."

"I certainly didn't see this woman on Saturday."

"I know. But that's not the point. What matters is that she set out with the intention of seeing you. . . . There were three of you, each with your regular days. François Paré's was

Wednesday, Courcel's Thursday night to Friday morning.
. . . Jean-Luc Bodard had no set day. . . .

"Most businessmen from the provinces who spend part of
the week in Paris return home on Saturday. You did not, because you had an arrangement to spend Saturday afternoons
with Mademoiselle Papet. . . .

"The concierge was aware of this, of course, which is why
she went to see you that day. . . . She didn't foresee that, as
you no longer had anything to keep you in Paris on Saturdays,
you would go back to Bordeaux on Friday night."

"Ingenious," remarked the lawyer, "but a bit flimsy as evidence to put before a jury, don't you think?"

The concierge, silent and motionless, seemed to fill the
room with her huge presence.

"I agree, Maître, but I am not relying on that alone. . . .
This gentleman here is Léon Florentin. . . . He has made a
full confession. . . ."

"I was under the impression that he was the chief suspect."

Florentin, shoulders hunched, hung his head, feeling that he
would never again be able to look anyone in the face.

"He is not the murderer," retorted Maigret, "but the intended victim."

"I don't understand."

But Lamotte understood. He started violently in his chair.

"It was at him that the gun was leveled in a threatening
gesture, designed to secure the return of certain compromising letters. . . . Monsieur Lamotte, however, is a very bad
shot, and, what's more, the weapon was unreliable. . . ."

The lawyer turned inquiringly to his client:

"Is this true?"

He had not been prepared for this turn of events. Lamotte
did not answer but, instead, glowered savagely at Florentin.

"It may help your case, Maître, to know that I am not convinced that your client fired the shot intentionally. He is a man accustomed to getting his own way, and when he meets with resistance he's liable to lose his temper. On this occasion, unfortunately, he had a gun in his hand, and it went off. . . ."

This time, the man with the limp was really shattered. He stared at Maigret with a dazed expression.

"I must ask you to excuse me for a moment. I shan't be long."

Maigret went through to the Law Courts and made his way up through the maze of corridors, as he had done on the previous Saturday. He knocked at the Examining Magistrate's door and went in to find him at his desk, immersed in a bulky file. His clerk was in the little room, carrying on the work of restoring order.

"It's all over!" announced Maigret, collapsing into a chair.

"Has he confessed?"

"Who?"

"Well . . . that fellow Florentin, I presume."

"He didn't kill anyone. . . . Even so, I shall require a warrant for his arrest. . . . The charge is attempted blackmail."

"And the murderer?"

"He's waiting in my office in company with his lawyer, Maître Bourdon."

"I can see trouble ahead! He's one of the most . . ."

"Don't worry, you'll find him most accommodating. I wouldn't go so far as to say that it was an accident, but there are a number of extenuating circumstances. . . ."

"Which of them . . ."

"Victor Lamotte, the man with the limp, Bordeaux wine-grower, respected member of the exclusive community of Les

Chartrons, where such matters as dignity and rank, not to mention moral rectitude, are not to be trifled with. . . .

"I'll spend this afternoon completing my report, and I hope to be able to let you have it by the end of the day. . . . It's almost lunchtime, and . . ."

"You're hungry, I expect."

"Thirsty!" admitted Maigret.

A few minutes later he was back in his office, where he handed over to Lapointe and Janvier the warrants signed by the Examining Magistrate.

"Take them up to Criminal Records for the usual formalities, and then see them to the cells."

Janvier, pointing to the concierge, who had risen to her feet, asked:

"What about her?"

"We'll attend to her later. . . . In the meantime, she'd better go back to the apartments. . . . The lodge can't be left unattended for ever."

She looked at him without expression. Her lips moved, and a little hiss escaped her, as when water is splashed on hot coals, but she did not speak. At last she turned toward the door and went out.

"I'll see you in a while, you two, in the Brasserie Dauphine."

Only as an afterthought did he realize how inconsiderate it had been of him to toss off this invitation to his men in the presence of those other two, who were about to be deprived of their liberty.

Five minutes later, standing at the bar of the familiar little restaurant, he gave his order:

"A beer . . . In the tallest glass you've got."

In thirty-five years he had not come across a single one of

the boys who had been his schoolmates at the Lycée Banville.

And when, at last, he did, it had to be Florentin of all people!

Épalinges, June 24, 1968